A Captain Hook, Crocodile,
& Wendy Darling Reimagining

DEVOURER OF MEN

NIKKI ST. CROWE

NIKKI ST. CROWE

Cover Design by Emily Wittig Designs

CONTENT WARNINGS

Graphic language, violence, abusive parent, verbally abusive parent/parent who uses derogatory language towards child, internal struggles with sexual identity/internal struggle of self due to parental abuse, graphic sexual content, mentions of spousal coma/death, blood drinking, captive/captivity, submission, talk of suicide

For a more comprehensive list of all of Nikki's work, please visit her website below.

https://www.nikkistcrowe.com/content-warnings

ACKNOWLEDGMENTS

This series would not be possible without the help of several readers.

First and foremost, thank you to Jeff for sensitivity reading Devourer of Men and helping me to accurately and respectfully portray the relationship between James Hook and the Crocodile. Any mistakes or inaccuracies that remain in this book are entirely my own.

A huge thank you to Rae and Ashleigh for beta reading and as always, keeping me above water!

And lastly, thank you to JV St. Crowe, my number one hype man and best friend. I appreciate all of the plot chats, character discussions, and endless support. If I was in a Why Choose Romance, you'd be my favorite husband.

To all the ones who think they're weak.
You're not.

A man of indomitable courage, it was said of him that the only thing he shied at was the sight of his own blood, which was thick and of an unusual colour.

— J.M. BARRIE

CHAPTER ONE
HOOK

I HAVE BEEN IN THE SEVEN ISLES FOR A VERY LONG TIME—PERHAPS longer than I dare to count. And yet it's been many, many years since I set foot on the island known as Everland.

Everland sits in the island chain between Pleasureland and Darkland, with Neverland to its north.

As far as islands go, it has always struggled with its identity. It wants to be respectable and powerful, but beneath the surface, it struggles to keep up with its own expectations.

In all the years since I've been here, it seems to have surrendered to its more deplorable urges.

The air stinks of soot and piss and the energy is just *off*.

I've been so consumed by my war with Peter Pan that I've barely looked up to notice how the Seven Isles might have changed.

"Aye?" the dockmaster says and peers up at me. Her eyebrows are thin and arching over her wide eyes in a perpetual state of alarm. Several tears in her tweed jacket have been stitched over in crimson thread, likely to match the shade of her bright red hair. There is a scent swirling around her that reminds me of burning sage and spiced tea.

"Beg your pardon?" I say because I'm not entirely sure where we were in the conversation.

"How long?" she repeats, her logbook open in hand, pen poised over the paper.

I glance at my ship tied halfway down the dock. My little sister Cherry and a handful of my men are staying over with it. I told Cherry I wanted her to watch out for the only place we have to call home, but really, I'm more worried for my sister's safety on land than I am on sea.

"A week to start," I answer.

"Very well." On the next dock over, two men shout at one another, then a pistol is drawn, a bullet fired. The dock-master ignores it and makes a note in her ledger.

"What's become of this place?" I mutter.

The woman looks up at me through the fringe of her red hair. "You want the truth or you want my opinion?"

"Is there a difference?"

"The monarchy," she says and slams the book shut. "Overrun by *malum vermes*." She makes a spatting sound aimed at the weathered dock.

Malum vermes. Evil worms. Everland has never liked calling a witch a witch. Probably because their monarchy was founded by witches and so they have to twist their own history to make themselves feel better about it.

Of all the islands in the island chain, Everland has the most superstition about evil. Last time I was here, they hung parcels of milk-soaked thistle over their windows, hoping to confuse the *vermes*.

"Evil worms, you say? So which one is it?"

"Huh?" Her brows sink just a fraction over her eyes.

"Your opinion or the truth?"

2

She shrugs and licks the end of her pen, wetting the ink again. "It'll be a hundred frongs for the week."

"A hundred! You must be joking."

"You don't like it, you can sail to another island."

"Bloody hell." I dig into the pocket of my jacket and produce the required fee. "For a hundred pieces, these docks should be paved in gold."

She snorts and takes the money. "Take it up with the queen, aye?"

I give her a tight smile. "I'll be sure to do that."

Someone calls her name and she hurries off, muttering about velveteen dandies.

I glance down at my velvet frock coat and start to question the choice to wear it. It's fine Winterland velvet that cost me more than I'd like to admit. It was meant to make a statement. One that says I am respectable and always in good form.

My father beat that sentiment into me at a young age.

We must always be perceived as superior.

But that only works if there is anyone to impress. Here it just shouts, "Hello. I am easy to rob."

With a grumble, I give the lapels a yank to straighten the jacket and start off down the dock.

NO. 3 HARBOR IS FOR TRAVELERS, SO THOSE MILLING ABOUT ARE IN no rush, many of them drunk.

I make my way into the heart of the city of South Avis. Avis is just on the edge of the Everland castle's curtain wall and from the right vantage point, you can see the castle's many turrets jutting up from the horizon line. Approaching dusk, it's too dark and too cloudy to see much, but it's not like I'm here for the monarchy anyway.

Smee confirmed that Wendy was last in the Everland High Tower Prison on the eastern edge of Avis, where the rocky shore and salty sea waves make it almost inhospitable. With all of the years that have passed since Peter Pan abandoned Wendy on Everland, I'm doubtful she's still there. There's no way anyone would survive the Tower for that long.

But it begs the question: if she is no longer a prisoner, then why didn't she send word? Why didn't she return to Neverland?

I'm not sure I want those answers yet. Best to leave those questions buried. I do, however, need some information before I can formulate a plan.

On the main road away from the docks, there's a cacophony of clacking horses' hooves and newspaper boys and street vendors calling out their wares. The air smells of roasted peanuts and horse shit.

The peanuts immediately make me think of *him*, my mortal enemy, and I move away from the scent as quickly as I can.

A carriage clatters past and I wait on the street corner for it to move along. Here the road forks in three directions. It's Second Street I want, where the road rises upward to the part of town known as UpHill. There should be plenty of rooms for rent there, and lots of drunks in taverns with loose lips.

When the hill crests and the street plateaus, I spot an overhanging sign for an inn called The Royal Suit. A red heart is hand painted at the top of the sign with thorny vines twining around the script lettering. I find the inside packed. Laughter and revelry and drinking and cavorting fills the smoky space. No one gives me a second glance. I make my way to the counter and am greeted by a woman half my age wearing a high-collared jacket with a red heart sewn over the chest.

"Greetings," the woman says a little distracted. There's a towel slung over her shoulder and an empty tray caught beneath her arm. "Something I can get for you?"

"A room, if you have one available."

"Of course." She sets the tray aside and wrestles out a thick tome to a bookmarked page in the center. It's a log of guests and rooms. "Name, sir?"

"Captain James Hook."

She writes in my name, then fetches an iron key and hands it over. "The room is around back. Number 11, sir. Dinner is served at half past six. You've already missed it tonight but I can put together a cold dish for you if you're hungry. It's venison stew. I'm Mills by the way. The cook and the innkeeper."

"It's a pleasure to meet you. I'm happy to wait for dinner tomorrow but thank you for the offer."

A man shouts the woman's name and she huffs out an exasperated breath. "If that'll be all?"

"Yes. Thank you."

There is a side door on the tavern that leads me to the alley and around back, away from the busier, noisier street. I find room number 11 and turn the key in the lock and hear the bolt thunk open inside.

The door creaks when I give it a push. It's not as big as my room at home and the first pang of longing takes me by surprise.

I cannot go home.

I have no home other than my ship.

Peter Pan made that clear enough.

There are three windows—two in front, and one on the west side of the room facing a scant back garden. The bed is a double with a lumpy mattress and threadbare quilt. It sits between two end tables with a lamp on each.

Water drips from a faucet in the washroom.

Beneath one of the windows, I pull out a rickety wooden chair at a round table and sit. Now that I'm at rest, I can feel the echoing sway of the ocean waves in my legs.

I lean against the chair and close my eyes and take in a deep breath.

What if I can't find Wendy Darling?

What if she doesn't want to be found?

Or worse—what if *he* finds her first?

Impossible. I left him unconscious on Neverland and got plenty of a head start.

The Crocodile couldn't possibly have beat me here.

Maybe he won't come at all.

Maybe I'll never see him again.

My gut clenches at the thought.

CHAPTER TWO

HOOK

It's been seven days and I've visited a half dozen taverns and spent countless coin greasing the lips of locals trying to get a morsel of information.

Any morsel.

And what do I have to show for it?

Nothing.

No one has heard of Wendy Darling.

No one has a contact within the Tower or within the prison guard.

I'm running into walls.

"Evening, Captain," Mills calls as I bypass the tavern's entrance and head around to the back. She's at one of the fence posts beating out a rug with a fluted cane. Dust clouds in the air. Sweat clings to several strands of her dark brown hair.

"Evening, ma'am."

"Mills," she corrects.

"Of course." I smile at her and keep walking. Despite it not even being suppertime, my head is pounding and my

7

vision unsteady after consuming three full glasses of Everland wine at the behest of Big Billy Green.

Despite his name, Big Billy was shorter than me by a full hand, but he drank like he was twice my size.

Big Billy Green may not be seeing over tall ledges, but he can drink the bottles off of each and every one of them.

I had heard he knew of Smee, which lead me to believe he might know Wendy.

But he was a dead end too.

Trudging up to my door, I yank the iron key from my pocket and loop the ring around the end of my hook, then twirl it as I think.

Perhaps I'm going about this wrong.

How many years has it been since I last saw Wendy? How old would she be now? No one ages the way mortals do in the island chain, but every island's magic is a little different. No one aged at all on Neverland. If I remember correctly, Everland's aging isn't too far off mortal aging.

The thought makes my stomach knot.

What if Wendy is already dead?

What if—

On my stoop, something crunches on the stone beneath my step.

I lift my boot and find a scattering of broken peanut shells.

The air freezes in my lungs and ice fills my veins.

No.

I whirl around, my heart thumping in my ears.

But no one is there.

Just Mills down the way beating her rug.

Whack. Whack.

The echo of horses' hooves from the street down the hill

mingles with the voices filtering out of open windows in the back of the tavern.

Where are you, Crocodile?

A breeze shifts through the courtyard and a skittering of leaves tumbles over the cobblestone.

Is he waiting for me inside the tavern?

Shadows move past the open windows, but I can't make out any of the faces.

I feel exposed, vulnerable. Which was exactly his intention, wasn't it?

My face flames, thinking of him watching me.

Fuck this and fuck him. He's taunting me. I won't fall for it.

I jam my key into the lock and push inside my room before thinking better of my haste.

What if he's waiting inside?

I brandish my hook like a weapon, my other hand on the butt of my pistol, just in case.

I check behind the door, and then edge into the washroom.

There's no one there.

A riot of laughter sounds from the tavern, causing me to jump. It's followed by the thumping of ale cups against solid wood tables.

With the toe of my boot, I slam the door shut and slide the bolt home, then pull one of the chairs into the center of the room and sit in it, facing the door, my pistol drawn in my lap.

When he comes, I will put a fucking bullet right between his eyes.

It feels like I've been sitting in this fucking chair for hours, but I have no way of knowing for sure. I tossed the clock out the window when I got here. All I know is there is darkness beyond my room and the revelry of the tavern has waned.

Minutes, hours, and no Crocodile.

I pace my room for a bit, trying to piece together my strategy while guessing at his.

What if he's already found Wendy and has gone to her? What if the peanut shells were just a ploy to keep me put?

I pour a drink after my back aches from the incessant pacing.

Glass in hand, I sit again and take a long pull. The alcohol helps drive away the chill in my gut, but it does nothing for the knotted tangle of nerves.

I'm exhausted, eyes heavy. But I'll stay up all night if I have to.

I drain the glass and then set it on the floor beside me and pull the pistol out again.

I feel better when the trigger is close at hand.

My eyes slip closed and I jolt awake a second later.

"Look alive," I mutter to myself, as if the sound of my own voice might break some of the tension threatening to close in.

How much longer until dawn? Four hours? Six?

Bloody hell, if only I didn't hate clocks so damn much.

I blink again as the exhaustion threatens to pull me under.

I can make it. I have to make it.

But I'm a fool for thinking so.

CHAPTER THREE
ROC

GETTING INSIDE THE CAPTAIN'S ROOM TAKES NO EFFORT AT ALL.

Mills, the innkeeper, was all too happy to give me an extra key when I told her I wanted to surprise my *very best friend* Captain James Hook.

"He looked like he was in need of one," Mills said. "A friend that is."

"Oh you have no idea," I'd answered.

When I push inside his room, I find him fast asleep in a rickety chair, his pistol limp in his hand. It isn't even the witching hour. The night is still young.

Leaving the door open, I cross to him and bend down. There is just a foot between us.

I take in a breath and come away with the scent of *pirate*. Rum and spice and old cigars.

His mouth is slightly ajar, the even breaths of sleep stealing past his lips.

He's shaved in the days since he left me.

Why?

He looks younger by half. Less rakish pirate, more merchant's son pretending to be something else.

11

Perhaps he's trying to hide from me, as if a beast like myself wouldn't know him in the dark.

There is an odd telling in my chest, a rising thump of my heart.

As I sailed here, I plotted all of the ways I'd make Captain Hook scream. But now that I'm standing in front of him, a scream doesn't seem quite as satisfying as a moan.

Perhaps I'll toy with him first. Perhaps I will enjoy it.

Quietly, I pull out the other chair from the table by the window and sit in a slouch.

The Captain doesn't move.

An oil lamp is still glowing on the bedside table and it fills the room with heavy, flickering light.

I pull out a handful of peanuts and crack one open and wait.

He comes to at half past midnight.

His lashes flutter against his cheeks and then he straightens, stretches out his legs, then remembers he should be on alert for very scary beasts and jolts upright.

When he spots me across the room, his instincts take over and he lifts the pistol and pulls the trigger.

The bullet hits the wall just over my shoulder and the plaster pebbles, plinking to the floor.

"You missed me, Captain," I say and toss a peanut shell. "I missed you too."

He's on his feet in a flash and because he's a little drunk and disoriented, I easily dodge out of his path.

I'm faster too. Being an ancient supernatural monster does have some perks.

He spins, eyes wide. "*You*," he says.

"Me," I answer and toss a peanut into my mouth, talking around the food. "Did you expect someone else? Don't make me jealous, Captain."

He barrels at me again and I let him corral me in the span of his arms.

He runs us back and I hit the opposite wall with an exaggerated *umph* and he presses into me.

His breath is hot, his eyes wide and bloodshot. "I'm going to kill you."

I laugh a little. "You keep saying that."

"Stop fucking smiling!"

"Maybe you should try smiling *more*, Captain." I flash him my teeth. "Perhaps I'll give you a reason to smile."

He scoffs and brings the sharp tine of his hook to my throat. It digs into my flesh, piercing skin, and when the first hot well of blood comes to the surface, I'm hard.

My heart is racing in my ears and my stomach is see-sawing and I fucking love it.

Will he kill me?

Death might be the sister of adventure. The heart surely thumps the same.

"Go on," I tell him. "Spill my blood and see what happens."

What will happen? I don't know. I'm inspired to find out.

"You lied to me," he spits out.

He's referring to Wendy Darling.

"You left me," I counter.

"I should have killed you while you lay unconscious."

I tsk-tsk. "And what would your father have thought of

that? Killing a man while he lay unconscious under your roof? *Poor form, Captain.*"

He grits his teeth and leans into me with more of his weight, pushing the hook deeper into my throat. But now that he's closer, there's no mistaking the bulge between my thighs.

I smile again.

All of the color drains from his face.

The tension fades from his body and he staggers back.

So that's how it is.

I'm not sure if I'm disappointed or delighted to have found a sore spot. I was just on a discovery mission and went with the first, most obvious one.

The Captain clearly has daddy baggage to unpack.

I do too, if I'm being honest. I just ignore mine better. Vane and I both. We grew up as the Darkland elite, fed a lie. We may be voracious beasts, but there are some things we could not swallow.

"Shut up," the Captain says limply.

"What purpose would that serve?"

He collapses into his chair, still a little disoriented, maybe a little defeated.

The unease in my chest...is that what guilt is supposed to feel like?

"Captain," I say.

He blinks up at me. His dark brown hair is ruffled, a little dry and wavy from the salty sea air. He's tired and worn and yes I think that might be guilt. I don't think I've ever felt a moment of guilt in my life except for when my sister died.

I go to the table and pour a shot of rum and hand it to him. "Drink."

There is a careful glint in his eye as he regards the glass, then checks the bottle behind him.

"I can assure you, Captain, if I wanted you dead, I would just eat you. Every tasty little bite."

He huffs and takes the offering and slings back the rum. He grimaces from the burn and then drags his knuckles over his mouth, wiping away the excess drops.

What beautiful, wet lips.

There is a throb low in my gut that I wish I could mistake for something other than desire.

This is no time for fucking and yet...

"What are you doing here?" he finally asks.

"A very stupid question when you clearly know the answer."

The glass lists in his hand, so I take it from him.

"She's not here," he says. "I've been searching for any clue for days and no one has heard of her."

"Perhaps you're looking in the wrong places and asking the wrong questions."

His brow furrows as he scowls up at me. "I know how to ask fucking questions."

I drag my chair to the center of the room and spin it around so I can sit on it backward and drape my arms over the back. "Your pride is getting in the way."

"It is not," he says, sharp with defensiveness.

"Ask me if I've found any clues," I tell him.

His gaze narrows more and his mouth turns down at the corners. "Have you?" The words come out quietly, burning with hope.

"Yes."

He sits forward. "How? When?"

"I am efficient. And persuasive."

"And you call me prideful."

"I said your pride was getting in the way. You can be prideful and not trip over it."

"Get to the point, beast."

I lean forward like I'm about to tell him a secret. He leans in too, like he's about to hear one.

"I met a girl last night," I start.

He rolls his eyes and sits back dramatically and I taste the tinge of jealousy on the air.

"And when I was buried balls deep in her sweet pussy—"

His jaw flexes with the grinding of his molars.

"—she told me a tale."

This is only partly true. I just like poking him to see how he may dance.

The truth is, I did meet a girl, but the information was acquired through the help of a banished fae queen who has the power to dig inside minds and extract worthwhile information.

There was no fucking involved.

"Let me guess," the Captain says. "She told you that you were the best lay she'd ever had?"

"Well that goes without saying."

He scoffs.

"I really do fuck like a god. Ask anyone."

"I would rather not."

"I could show you."

He fidgets, shifts his weight, and the chair takes note of his agitation, punctuating it with a loud squeak. His face burns hot. I think I quite like him without facial hair. There's nowhere for him to hide.

"Quit trying to derail the conversation," he says. "Wendy. Stick to Wendy."

I spread out my long legs and the Captain's gaze follows

the movement and I catch him eyeing my crotch. "The girl told me a friend of hers had a grandmother who spent time in the Tower many years ago and that she shared a cell with a woman named Wendy."

The oil lamp catches a draft and the flame dances, the light flickering across the Captain's face as his eyes jump back to mine. "Wendy Darling?"

"Yes."

The chair creaks again. "Is she still alive?"

I shrug. "I'm to see the girl—" I pull out my pocket watch and the Captain winces at the ticking, "—in an hour and ten."

"At this ungodly hour?"

"Everland does not sleep."

"Where?"

I cluck my tongue at him. "You made it perfectly clear that you didn't want to work together, Captain. After all, you left me unconscious back on Neverland and sailed off into the sunset, absent a beast." I stand. "So I really must be going."

"Wait." He stands too and reaches out for me, catching me by the wrist.

I look down at his skin on mine. His is smooth and unmarred and a little baked by the sun. Mine is pale and storied in ink and scars.

We are a dichotomy, the Captain and I. He wants to forget who he is and I am afraid I might not remember who I was.

"I'm sorry," he says quietly and frowns at his own admission, as if it's surprised him, sneaking past his lips, traitorous little words they are.

Do I care if he's sincere? Do I care if we search for

Wendy together or apart? It might be fun to make a game of it.

But because I like torturing prideful men, I say, "What was that? I couldn't hear you."

"Christ." He rolls his eyes and drops my arm. "I'm sorry I left you unconscious! I'm sorry I sailed away without you. Was that loud enough for you?"

"Well you don't have to shout, Captain."

He points his hook at me. "I change my mind. I'm back to murdering you."

I laugh and turn for the door. "Come, Captain. Let's get a drink and some food while we wait for our meeting. I promise to be a good boy and only eat what's on my plate." I wink at him over my shoulder. His face is pink again and I think I've never seen anything so fucking delectable.

With a ragged exhale, the Captain turns down his oil lamp and follows me out the door.

CHAPTER FOUR
HOOK

Walking through the busy streets of Everland's Dock District at this late hour, when only degenerates and drunks and rogues are about, one would think the Crocodile would fit right in.

Somehow he still manages to stand apart.

I think it's in the casual absence of fear and wariness. As if he has no enemy and no equal here.

On the next street corner, a fight breaks out and several men shove one another, throwing punches. A fourth brandishes a knife. He slashes. Someone shouts. Another man goads them on.

The Crocodile saunters past, barely glancing over as he upends a nut into his open mouth. I'm a few paces behind him and the hollowed shells of his peanuts crunch beneath the soles of my boots.

"Where is this meeting?" I ask him.

"The Tipping Well," he answers, dusting off his hand and lighting a cigarette. To our left, one of the fighting men stabs another in the gut. I lurch back as blood paints the cobblestones. The Crocodile walks through it, leaving behind a trail of bloody footprints.

In the distance, a whistle belonging to the Guardwatch blows in the night.

Everland has become a place of mayhem and chaos on the outskirts, where the monarchy can turn a blind eye.

Just who is running this country anyway? The dockmaster mentioned a queen but Everland has never been a forward-thinking kingdom. Women don't typically rule here.

We turn left at the next intersection and a block ahead, the printed sign for The Tipping Well swings from an iron hook above the door.

Years past, before Roc took my hand, I'd visit Everland from time to time to strike deals with the merchants. Pirating was at an all-time high and companies were losing shipments day after day. It was in their best interest to ship with a privateer like myself, one who could safely transport, not because he was cutthroat, but because he secretly controlled the shipping lines and the pirates who pirated it.

It was perhaps poor form, but I knew how the merchants operated — they made their fortunes at the expense of their laborers. No one was morally sound, including myself.

The Tipping Well sits on the edge of the Merchant District and is just a ten-minute walk from the Ministry of Merchants. Because of that, it was a popular meeting destination. I've been to the tavern on many occasions. I never would have thought to look here for information on a prisoner.

The Crocodile takes a hit of his cigarette and exhales smoke. It clouds over his shoulder and when we come up on the thick wooden door of the tavern, he drops the cigarette and crushes the embers beneath his boot.

He looks over at me. "Before we go in, there are a few rules about this place that you absolutely must follow."

I frown at him. "Since when do you abide by rules?"

"One: *behave*."

"The bloody hell do you—"

"Two: *don't drink the wine. No matter what.*"

"Why not?"

"And three: *don't ever say thank you.*"

"Oh please. Being polite is good form."

"Captain." He tilts his head and chastises me with a look like I'm a meal that has bleated too loudly.

Heat bristles across my chest. "I swear to the fucking gods I'm going to—"

He winks at me, swats me on the ass, and steps inside.

I really am going to murder him. I mean it this time. More than any of the other times before.

The Tipping Well is not how I remember it either. The rickety wooden furniture has been replaced with sturdy Winterland oak, the seats done in rich emerald leather and tacked down with hand-wrought bronze nails, the chiseled style of the heads glittering like cut diamonds.

Above, the oil lanterns that used to smoke and stink up the place are now electrical lights, the bulbs' glare softened by ivory cloth shades. And hanging from beam to beam are string lights that glimmer in the vaulted shadows of the ceiling.

NIKKI ST. CROWE

The air smells of roasted meat, sugared nuts and sweet tobacco.

A fire crackles on the stone hearth just inside the door and a three-man band plays on the raised dais beside it.

I take in a deep breath and immediately feel...*odd*.

The Crocodile makes his way through the tavern and several patrons call out hello to him.

I sway on my feet, head buzzy, stomach light.

"Captain."

This place is warm and cozy and am I smiling? I think I'm smiling. I rarely have a reason to smile other than—

"Captain."

I blink when the Crocodile snaps his fingers in front of my face.

"Why do I feel so...good? Do I feel good?" I giggle.

"Come." He hooks his arm around my shoulders and draws me into his warm embrace. He smells like wild nights and moonlight.

"You smell good," I tell him. "Everything is good."

"Perhaps this was a mistake." He drives me to the rear, to a half-circle booth tucked in a dimly lit corner and shoves me onto the seat. "Sit."

I laugh and scoot along the bench. "Bloody hell I feel amazing."

A server appears at our table wearing a shimmering gold dress and butterflies in her hair. Her eyes are an unnatural shade of amethyst, and she flutters her lashes at the Crocodile. "Where ye been?" she asks him.

"Oh Briar," he coos. "I can't be everywhere at all times."

"Last time ye were here, ye left me bed before the midnight hour. Ye promised."

"You left her bed?" I lean into the Crocodile and laugh. "That sounds like him," I tell her.

She nods at me but speaks to him. "Is this your tithe then?"

"Absolutely not." The Crocodile's voice shifts, edged in warning.

"He's drunk already." Her hair butterflies lift with a soft flap of wings. "Can't hold his merry?"

"He's starved for it, apparently." The Crocodile nudges me. "I need you to snap out of it."

"I'm behaving," I say to him and smile. "Rule number one."

He rolls his eyes at me. Bloody hell he has the fucking best eye roll. So sexy and rolly.

The Crocodile fishes out several thin bars of gold and sets them on the table. They're stamped on the top edge with a language I immediately recognize as fairy.

"My tithe," he says. "Get him bread and ale. Quick about it, Briar."

The butterfly girl scoops up the bars and then flits away.

"Captain," he says.

"Crocodile," I say. "Beast. Beastly man."

He groans and then his gaze wanders away, watching the movement of the people in the room. All of them are a blur to me. There is only him and the sharp cut of his black jacket, the way it hugs his shoulders, the stiff collar standing up along his jawline. The way that jaw clenches as he watches the tavern.

The way he looks like a dark moon feels, like a mystery, like a secret.

Briar reappears with one hand hooked through the handles of two ale mugs. In her other hand is a plate of toasted and buttered bread. She sets all in front of us. "Anything else? Wine perhaps?"

"Yes," I say.

"No," the Crocodile says and gives me an admonishing look.

"Very well. I'm starving. This looks divine. Thank—" The Crocodile slaps his hand over my mouth.

"Rule number three, remember?" His eyes bore into mine. He's serious now and worried. There is a pinch of it between his dark brows. A heaviness that I wish to relieve him of.

Three rules. Yes. Follow the rules.

I give him a nod and he pulls his hand away.

"That will be all, Briar," he tells the butterfly girl and she disappears.

The band switches tunes and the tavern's energy shifts.

"Eat." The Crocodile shoves the bread in front of me.

I'm not used to people ordering me around but coming from the Crocodile...I should hate it but I don't.

I take a bite. The butter is rich and infused with garlic and rosemary. The bread tastes like it was freshly baked today. It's crunchy around the crust, soft in the middle.

While I eat and suck down the ale, the Crocodile scans the room again and says nothing. He's not even eating his damn peanuts.

When the bread is gone, sense returns to me and the first rational thought I have is embarrassment, then anger.

"Did you drug me?" I ask him.

His eyes are still on the room. "It's the magic."

"The what?"

He finally looks at me. A lock of his hair falls over his forehead. I want to swipe it back. I want to touch him so badly it hurts.

"A year ago, several Pleasureland fae bought The Tipping Well. Now the place is infused with fae magic.

Most people just feel calmer when they walk in the door. Keeps them drinking, spending coin. But other people, people who may or may not be pent up with unspent energy and emotion, fall much deeper."

I scowl at him. "What are you saying?"

"I'm saying that you need to loosen up a bit or you'll end up licking the boot of one of the fae proprietors before the night is over. Or worse," he adds.

"You could have warned me."

"I did." He leans back against the booth and spreads his arms out. "You just chose to ignore me."

"I think what you mean is I chose not to trust you."

"Don't make that mistake again."

I am acutely aware of his arm behind me, the nearness of his inked skin, the way he takes up space that should not be his, but that he still somehow owns.

He could have let me fall for the fae magic. But he didn't.

Why not?

I look over at him. He's shifted his left arm, hand curled around the mug of ale, but he hasn't touched it. There is tension in his body despite the languid way he slouches in the booth.

When we first walked in, all I could smell was the food and the magic, but now that we're alone back here, all I can smell is him.

Spice and musk and darkness and urgency.

I'm overwhelmed by him.

Is it the magic again? Did he know this would happen? His way of getting back at me for leaving him on Neverland?

"What happens when you drink the wine?" I ask.

His gaze cuts to me. There is a flash of depravity in his eyes and then it's gone.

"You lose your inhibitions," he answers.

"Is that not what all alcohol does?"

"You don't get drunk, Captain." He leans in closer so he can whisper in my ear. "You just get bold."

A shiver races down my spine.

I've sailed the seas of the Seven Isles. I've visited five of the seven islands. Fought other pirates and killed many more.

And yet some days I am aware that I am driven mostly by fear.

Fear of who I am.

Fear of who I'm not.

Fear of what happens when I face myself in the mirror.

To be bold is to be truthful and I am built of lies.

IT TAKES ME ANOTHER SLICE OF BUTTERED BREAD AND A SECOND glass of ale before the fogginess of the tavern's magic fades. The entire time, the Crocodile watches the room and ignores me. Which is just as well. I'm afraid of what I might do if provoked by him.

Despite this, I am endlessly fascinated by him and I can't seem to tear my eyes away.

He's slouched in the booth now, propped up on an elbow, one leg stretched out beneath the table, the other kicked up on the bench.

Once upon a time, he was everything I feared and hated.

I still do, hate him that is. I no longer fear him.

Or at least, I no longer fear him in the same way.

Wait, what am I saying? There is no gray area with the Crocodile. I must remind myself of that. I must keep my wits about me when he's around.

He tips his head back and checks on me for the first time in so many minutes.

The tavern lights wash him in diffused gold and I find myself drawn to the bow of his lips, that sharp, dangerous mouth. My gut soars like I'm riding a ship-killing wave in the middle of a dark stormy night.

It's obscene, how intimate and provocative he is even in repose.

If I were on my ship, I would be clutching the railings, holding on for dear life. That's how I feel right now, like the world is heaving beneath me. I'm both exhilarated and terrified of it.

"Captain," he says and reaches over, his hand on my thigh, so fucking close to my cock.

I lurch away. My knee knocks the underside of the table and the cutlery rattles against the plate.

The Crocodile frowns at me, but the expression is laced with amusement.

"Where were you just now?" He's sitting up again, watching me with an intensity that burns.

"What the bloody hell do you mean? I'm right here."

Sweating. Burning. Hard like stone.

He makes a quick slide down the bench until we are pressed together.

I swallow.

"'Lies My Captain Told Me.'" He runs his tongue over his bottom lip, trailing it with wetness. He laughs. "That's the title of my future memoir."

I snort and reach for my drink. Anything to distract me, to hide the tremor in my hands.

My captain. *MY* captain?

He leans over. Scrutinizes me closer and the ocean heaves again.

"Is there anything as sexy as a squirming ship's captain?" His mouth curves into a smile. "I think not."

Christ.

He's playing with me and I'm dancing for him like a fucking puppet.

"Shut up," I tell him because I can't think of anything more sufficient.

"Make me, Captain," he challenges, bracing his tongue on the sharp tine of his incisor. "I can think of one very fun way for you to shut me up."

"Bloody hell." I grip my drink harder. I'm shocked the clay hasn't cracked.

"I'm talking about blow jobs, Captain."

"Yes, I know."

"Do you want to know what I think is funny about blow jobs?"

Yes. "Not particularly." I take a long swig of the ale wishing it was something stronger. Is the rum safe in this place? Why are we only drinking ale? I gesture to Briar. She nods and lifts a finger indicating it'll be a minute.

I look over at Roc. He's still staring at me, but he's shifted a little so that the fabric of his shirt is tight across his middle. I know beneath it lay hard packed muscle and ridges so deep, I could pour my glass over him, watch the liquor fill up the valleys. I could drink from those rivers.

Suddenly I'm fantasizing about being on my knees in front of him, worshipping every inch of his body.

How did we get on the subject of blow jobs anyway?

The Crocodile cracks a peanut and I can't help but

wince at the loud break of the shell. "Open up," he says, and rolls the peanut between thumb and forefinger.

"I'm not a circus animal."

"Open your fucking mouth, Captain."

I breathe out through my nose, but then do as he says.

He tosses me the peanut and I play for him, catching the peanut easily. It breaks between my molars and the richness of the nut fills my mouth.

He watches me more. He watches me swallow it. He watches me as if he's satisfied.

"Blow jobs are a power dichotomy," he says and sits up straighter, dusting the shell from his hands. "Most people think that being on your knees and getting railed in the face is a position of submission. But a man is never more vulnerable than he is when his cock is in someone's mouth. Especially a mouth with sharp teeth."

He smiles at me and I have to readjust in my chair as my cock stirs. He knows what he's doing. The Crocodile always knows what he's doing, always has the moment in his firm grip.

This is not how I imagined this night going. It's gotten away from me. Or maybe I have gotten away from myself.

"Oh look," he says and nods at the front door. "She's here."

She? Right. The girl we're to meet to gather information about Wendy's whereabouts.

I've completely forgotten.

How quickly the world blurs when I am tempted by a beast.

CHAPTER FIVE
ROC

Palametto is a thief, but not a very good one. She's wanted on every island for various crimes, most of them pick-pocketing. Still, I make sure to keep the table between us as she pulls up a chair and sits down.

She's a curvy girl, on the shorter side, with a long braid of brown hair and a dusting of freckles across her face. She's the kind of girl that given the right training could be an excellent thief. There's nothing about her that stands out. She could blend into any crowd.

I catch her eyeing the black rock hanging around my neck and snap my fingers at her. "My eyes are up here."

She smiles at me looking as innocent as can be. She leans into the table, hunching her shoulders forward affording me, and the Captain, a view of her cleavage.

I may have been lying when I told the Captain I'd fucked her friend, but I'm not above using my body to get what I want. However, I'm not about to fuck Palametto. Not my type. Too many freckles. That saying, that freckles are the mark of the devil? Not entirely untrue.

Besides it's not my dick she's after — it's money.

"Pay the girl," I tell the Captain.

"What?" He scowls at me. "Is that the only reason you brought me?"

I ignore him and press a thumb into a peanut on the table. The shell cracks.

The Captain fishes out several dukets from his pocket and slides them across the table to the girl.

"That it?" She turns up her nose at the silver.

The Captain looks at me. "Don't you have more of those—"

I kick him beneath the table. He lets out a dramatic umph.

Palametto raises a brow.

I keep my expression blank. Don't want the thief knowing I have fairy gold in my pocket.

We stare at each other for several long beats, then she says, "Throw in the rock and we'll call it good."

"You lay one finger on my rock," I tell her, "and I'll devour you whole."

"Is that some kind of sexual innuendo?"

The Captain brings his hook up and sets it on the table. The metal clangs loudly against the wood. The girl glances at it before looking up at the Captain's face, asking a question that I think she already knows the answer to.

"If you'd like my advice, young lady, I wouldn't tempt him," he says.

My attention wanders to the Captain, to the grim line of his mouth. I have to suppress a shiver, hearing him talk about me like this: a foe that should not be ignored.

The Captain is sexy AF when he's flattering me.

Palametto rakes her teeth over her ruby red lips. "Fine. The silver will do."

"Excellent choice," I tell her around a mouthful of nuts. "Now, what can you tell us about Wendy Darling?"

Briar comes over and takes the girl's drink order. The Captain orders a bottle of rum. When I give him a surprised look he screws up his mouth at me as if he's challenging me to tell him he's not allowed.

I'm not going to stop him. A drunk Captain is a lot more fun than a sober one. Even if I do get a great amount of joy out of telling him what to do.

"My mamaw used to talk about a girl she spent time with in prison," Palametto says. "This was a long, long time ago, right? They were in the same cell in the Tower."

"What was your grandmother in for?" I ask, because details matter and because a bloodthirsty granny is exactly my type. Unless she has freckles.

"Killing a man."

I raise a brow. "And did she?"

"Of course. Mamaw was a Cutty and she slit the throat of anyone who got in her way."

"I didn't think the Cuttys let women into their ranks."

"You don't tell Mamaw no."

"I like this granny of yours. Go on."

"In prison, she and the girl were in together about a month before the girl, Wendy, was taken for execution."

Hook's eyes widen. "What the bloody hell for?"

The girl shrugs. "I think Mamaw said something about Peter Pan? Everland sees anyone with ties to Pan as automatically an enemy of the court."

There's no way they went through with it. The timeline wouldn't match up with Wendy's pregnancy and later birth.

Briar returns. The Captain wastes no time uncorking his bottle and pouring himself a drink. His heart is beating erratically. I can hear it even over the music, even over the din.

"What happened after that?" the Captain asks.

I grab the bottle from him and take a long draw from it. He scowls at me, but it's short-lived when Palametto goes on. He's hungry for any detail about Wendy and I'm a little envious of it.

"They tried to execute Wendy by hanging. But she just dangled there for over an hour, refused to die. The way Mamaw told it, the Viscount at the time stepped in and took Wendy home with him. Real asshole that one was, and he coveted rare treasures. The rumors started then that Wendy was a *vermis* and the Viscount tried to sell her. Didn't get very far though."

The Captain takes the bottle back from me. "What's that supposed to mean?"

She leans in conspiringly. "The Viscount passed away."

I lean in too. "Got himself dead, you mean?"

"Probably. Seems awfully convenient, doesn't it?"

"What about Wendy?" the Captain asks.

The girl shrugs. "Disappeared after that."

He collapses against the booth. "You must be joking."

"Not. Sorry." Palametto slings back her drink in one long gulp, then runs the back of her hand over her mouth, mopping up the last dregs.

The Captain presses his thumb and forefinger to the bridge of his nose.

"Is there anything else you can tell us?" I ask.

The girl gives me a begging smile. "Perhaps you and I go back to my room and have a little fun and we can see if anything shakes loose."

The Captain is now glaring at her.

"Please accept my apologies." I reach across the table

and pat her hand. "I plan on fucking him tonight so I must decline."

The Captain sputters and it takes everything in me not to laugh out loud.

"He is not!" he tells the girl, and then he looks at me. "You are not!"

"Don't blame you," she says to me, ignoring Hook while talking about him. "He's a fine handsome dandy."

"That he is."

"I'm right here," he grumbles.

"If you change your mind…" Palametto adds.

"I'm sure I could find you." I'm sure I won't.

She winks and then leaves us.

I drag the bottle of rum back over and take a swig. Pleasureland fae aren't known for their discerning taste in rum, but it's serviceable. Sweet, spicy, with a sharp burn on the way down.

"I don't know if the fairy magic has gotten to your head," the Captain says, leaning into me, "but you are not —" he lowers his voice "—fucking me tonight."

"Oh? Did you want to fuck me instead?"

He grumbles to himself and steals the bottle back. "You are a fucking menace, do you know that?"

"Of course I do. I'm very good at it."

"You think you're good at everything."

"Nonsense. I'm very bad at knitting."

He snorts.

The band takes a request from the growing crowd and an upbeat Winterland tune fills the tavern. Several patrons partner off and swing around in a choreographed dance known as the Allemande. Those gathered around clap in time with the strumming of the giant bass.

The Captain picks up his forgotten bread and rips off a piece. "I thought you wanted to find Wendy."

"I do."

"Then why are you sitting here, playing all of this like it's a game?"

"Everything is a game, Captain. The sooner you pick your game piece, the quicker you can win."

I sense some of the tension come out of him as he slumps against the bench. "Meeting that girl," he says. "I don't feel like she got us anywhere closer to finding Wendy."

I watch the crowd. Palametto has already disappeared into it. I check that my rock is still hanging around my neck.

"We did get something out of it. Wendy was here. They tried to kill her. They couldn't."

"That can't be right though. Wendy was mortal when she came to the Isles. There's no way she'd survive an hour of hanging."

My mind conjures the image of Wendy struggling against a noose, legs kicking at nothing, and it makes me fucking irate. I was hung once. It did not go well for the executioner.

"We need to find out more about the Viscount's death," I say, thinking aloud. "If he did take Wendy in, she would have been considered his property at the time of death. We just need to figure out who took his assets."

The Captain snorts. "Good luck to us."

"Captain, pessimism does not become you."

"Oh fuck off."

I laugh and snatch the rum from him again. "You're sexy when you're angry."

"Shut up. Stop flirting with me." He avoids looking

directly at me. But I notice him surreptitiously readjusting himself.

I slide down the bench, press my body against the Captain's. He shrinks away, but I grab him by the arm and keep him against me.

There is a moment where all of the tension rushes out of his body and he slumps against me, his thigh pressing against mine. He is warm and soft and hostile. All of my favorite things.

He frowns at me. "Is this also part of the game, beast?"

"Take a deep breath," I tell him.

"Why?" He regards me warily.

"You're no good to me if you're pent up."

"I'm not."

"You are."

"I am not pent up."

"Take a deep breath."

I want to mold him, make him bend to me. I want to watch him pull away the mask and become something else: *himself*.

"Go on, Captain."

He huffs out and then inhales deeply.

"Again," I tell him.

He takes another deep breath, lungs expanding.

I see the moment the fairy magic seeps into his bloodstream. See the moment the anxiety and the apprehension fades.

"Better?" I ask him.

He looks at me a little starry-eyed. "This is dangerous," he slurs.

"Why?"

"Because I..." He closes his eyes, swallows hard.

"Because you what?"

"Because I don't feel afraid right now." His eyes pop open and focus on me. "I should be afraid of you. I should have my wits about me when you are near."

"I won't hurt you, Captain," I promise him. "I find no pleasure in your pain."

His hook twists in his lap. "You did once."

"Sure. A long time ago."

"What changed?"

Everything, I think. "Now I find pleasure in watching you squirm."

"A different kind of torture." His voice is a grumble of annoyance, but I catch the bulge between his legs growing larger.

"Why don't you give in to me," I tell him. "And let me repent for what I did to you all those years ago."

He sucks in another deep breath, this time of his own accord, and lets his eyes stay closed a heartbeat, two, three. I can hear the blood pumping through his veins, the temptation beating at the back of his tongue.

When his eyes pop open again, he's looking right at me, then at my mouth, at the crocodile teeth tattooed across my neck.

I'm not sure I desire redemption, but the way he's looking at me, like he's terrified I'm a lie, a Crocodile hiding beneath the muck, teeth ready to snap, makes me question myself.

I am not a decent man.

But I suppose even a beast such as myself is allowed to do one decent thing.

I laugh and drop his arm and slide away. "You're drunk," I tell him. "And I'm hungry. If this is a game, I tire of it. Why don't we get out of here and find some decent food and rum?"

He deflates.

There is an unfamiliar feeling in my throat, a tightening that spiderwebs across my chest. I am stuck in it and I cannot get out.

"Very well," he says and takes the rum bottle by the neck. "I know a place better than this. Follow me, beast."

I slide out of the booth and trail the Captain out the door.

CHAPTER SIX
HOOK

W͟HEN͟ I͟ H͟I͟T͟ T͟H͟E͟ F͟R͟E͟S͟H͟, C͟O͟O͟L͟ A͟I͟R͟ O͟F͟ N͟I͟G͟H͟T͟, T͟H͟E͟ S͟W͟E͟A͟T͟ gathering at the back of my neck chills, and I have to brace to hide the shiver threatening to shake my entire body.

I am running from the Crocodile. Again. But this time he's following close behind and I want him to chase me. I want him to catch me.

Bloody fucking hell.

Roc comes up beside me, a cigarette caught between his lips. He hunches, one hand cupped around the end of the cigarette while he flicks a flame to life with a lighter in his other.

The tobacco crackles.

When the cigarette is burning, Roc flicks the lighter closed on his thigh. It is a definitive snap in the night.

He eyes me as he takes a long drag, curling his finger around the end caught in his mouth.

I told him I knew a better place for food but that was just an excuse to run.

Now he's looking at me expectantly.

I can't breathe.

"Which way?" he asks, expelling a breath of smoke.

I start forward, directionless.

Roc is two steps behind, but the smoke of his cigarette curls around me like a taunting ghost.

I turn down a street.

He follows.

The street narrows and the din of the tavern fades behind us.

"Are you sure you know where you're going?" he asks.

"Of course I do."

I don't.

Bloody hell I don't. There must be something right around the next corner, surely.

Except the street gets darker, filthier.

The only sound is that of the scampering of rats and the scrap of the Crocodile's boots on the stone.

"Captain," he starts, but I cut him off, glancing at him over my shoulder.

"I know where I'm going!"

The glowing ember of his cigarette renders him in sinister shadows. He fills his lungs with smoke, but he's not looking at me. He's looking past me.

"I would duck," he says, holding the smoke in his lungs.

"What?"

He breathes out. "Duck, Captain."

Behind me, there is the sound of something hard cutting through the air.

I turn around just in time to see a wooden club flying at my face.

The hit sends shockwaves through my skull, down my neck, all the way down to my feet. My bones vibrate with it.

The world spins and I can taste blood in my mouth.

Blood. Mine. I'm bleeding.

The panic is immediate.

I grasp around for something, anything, and when my vision realigns I realize I'm on the cobblestone.

Get up.

Onto all fours.

The street sways again and I squeeze my eyes shut, spit blood on the stone.

Don't look. Can't look.

Using the brick wall of the nearest building, I slowly climb to my feet. To my right, Roc is surrounded by three men. Two are brandishing wooden clubs, the third has an open blade, the steel finding a ray of moonlight to glint sharply like a grin.

The men circle him as he stands in the middle casually smoking his cigarette.

Does nothing ruffle him?

"Empty yer pockets."

The hoarse voice pulls my attention away. I find the man who hit me standing to my left, club slung over his shoulder.

My ears are ringing, my head pounding.

"What?" I croak.

"Empty. Yer. Pockets, eh!"

"Captain?"

I don't take my eyes off the man with the club even though I'm currently seeing two of him and finding it difficult to decide which one is real. "Yes?"

"Can I trust you to handle yourself?" the Crocodile asks.

"I don't need your help," I tell him, a little offended that he thinks I might.

"Good."

"You think you can take us, do you?" the one with the blade says.

The Crocodile laughs. His laughter bounces off the walls. "Our meeting was actually fortuitous."

"Oh yeah? How's that?"

"Because I'm hungry." The Crocodile lunges. He grabs the thief nearest him, gets his hands on the man's bald head and twists.

The sound of his neck snapping echoes through the street and it wakes up the others.

My assailant swings again, but I duck this time. The motion throws me off balance and I slam back into the wall, the club hitting stone just a few inches above me.

I dart away, my coat flapping at my hips, revealing the pistol strapped to my side.

The man's face falls when he spots it and he comes straight at me taking up a fistful of my jacket. We crash into the opposite wall and pain radiates through my ribcage.

I reach for the pistol, but the man swipes at me, then follows with a sharp elbow jab, knocking the wind out of me.

I cough. Sputter. Gasp for air.

Behind the man, a glowing cigarette appears, then Roc is raising his arm, my rum bottle caught in his grip.

My eyes widen. The man catches the change in my expression a second too late.

Roc brings down the liquor bottle and smashes it against the man's knobby head. The glass shatters, rum spraying everywhere.

The man's eyes roll back in his head and his club hits the stone with a loud clatter.

Roc catches him before he hits the stone, wrests back his head, exposing his throat, and then sinks his teeth into the meaty flesh.

Air finally trickles down my throat.

Roc drinks. And drinks. And drinks.

The man is boneless and dead within seconds and the Crocodile drops him unceremoniously, his body folding in on itself, slumped over like a forgotten doll.

The Crocodile lets out a satisfied sigh before looking over at me. "I thought you said you could handle yourself?"

Back against the wall, I straighten the lapel of my jacket. "I had it handled."

"Looked like it." He smiles at me, then drags his tongue through the blood clinging to his wet mouth. "He catch you with a knife?"

"What?"

He gestures at my midsection. I look down to find my shirt slowly eaten away by the spread of dark blood.

"Oh fuck."

The world shifts again. My heart kicks up and knocks against my ribs as my stomach rolls.

I slump against the wall, gasping for air a second time within so many minutes.

"I forgot," Roc says and comes to my side, catching me before I fall. "You can't stand the sight of your own blood."

White stars edge my vision. "I...can't breathe."

"Captain," he says.

I claw at my neck. Everything hurts. Everything is pulled taut inside of me, ready to snap.

"Captain."

I'm going to die. I'm going to die from panic, from my own sins.

Of course I would bleed darkest black.

Of all the nights and all the things...

The Crocodile yanks off his jacket and tosses it onto a pile of crates. Then he's tearing into his shirt, turning it into strips.

"Arms up," he orders me, but I can barely hear him over the loud thumping of my heart. He makes do, tying the strips of fabric around my wound while I gasp for air.

"That better?" he asks me.

I shake my head, turning red, eyes bulging. "I...can't..."

With an impatient grumble, the Crocodile pulls me against him and suddenly his mouth is on mine.

He is hungry and insistent and I open for him without thinking. He breathes life into me, fills my lungs and the world stops swaying.

The pain fades, the panic too.

Have I already died?

When he pulls back, I blink up at him. There is blood smeared across his face and I can taste the remnants of it on the tip of my tongue.

But that's not my blood, so it doesn't matter.

"Better now?" the Crocodile asks.

"You kissed me," I blurt like a drunk idiot.

He smiles. "It was a calculated distraction."

It worked.

Except I can hear my father's voice in my head.

Poor form, boy. Cavorting with the enemy.

I have spent the night with a beast, tempted by his mouth.

But if giving into him was so bad, why am I buzzing? Why do I finally feel alive?

I am a wayward man that's been shoved into an empty room. Empty save for one table and on that table is a little red button that reads DO NOT PUSH.

In that room, temptation breathes the same air. It paces the same stretch of floorboards. Back and forth with me, whispering in my ear.

Push the button.

Push the button.

I am the wayward man and the Crocodile is the button.

And oh how I desire to push it.

He wipes the blood from his face with the backside of his shirtsleeve. "We should go before the Guardwatch—"

I close the distance between us, crash into him and kiss him.

CHAPTER SEVEN
ROC

FOR ONCE, I'M THE ONE TAKEN BY SURPRISE.

I am not often surprised.

I am not often delighted by being surprised.

It's like opening a present meant for someone else and finding exactly the thing you wanted all along.

Now it's mine and now I will not give it back.

I wrap my hand around the back of the Captain's neck, taking control, and swing him around, pressing him into an alcove where paint peels from an unmarked door. The old wood creaks.

The Captain lets out a startled gasp and I swallow the sound.

He groans a second later, his tongue finding mine. I can taste the sweetness of the rum still lingering on him.

He's hard against me in an instant, his cock digging into the curve of my thigh.

The present is mine. I'm ready to fucking tear into the wrapping.

"Captain," I say when his grasp on my bicep tightens like he wants to tear into me too. "If I had known killing men for you would get you so horny, I would have slaughtered a village a long time ago."

"Shut up," he tells me.

I laugh into him and grab him roughly between the legs.

He breaks the kiss, arches against the door, trying to get away, panting out a huff of panic now that I have him by the balls.

Fucking delightful.

"We can't stay here," I tell him.

There are four corpses behind us and they're starting to make a mess of the cobblestones. The Guardwatch might not patrol this part of town with enthusiasm, but someone will happen past eventually.

The Captain nods. "Let's go back to my room."

I lick my lips. His eyes flare to life, following the drag of my wet tongue.

"Tell me, Captain, are you sober? Do you know what you're asking for? Because once you have it, there is no turning back."

"Are you insinuating you're a drug?"

I smile showing all my sharp teeth. "I'm insinuating that once you have me, you will not be the same after."

He snorts. "You are an arrogant prick."

I squeeze him harder and he hisses, but there is an unmistakable answer in his cock. So the Captain likes pain as much as pleasure?

Or maybe he likes to be tested. And controlled.

"Answer the fucking question."

"Yes," he says quickly, then scowls at me as if he has the moment in hand. He doesn't. He will never have control with me.

"I'm sober," he says. "I know what I'm doing."

But does he?

No one knows what they're getting when they climb into my bed.

"When's the last time you had a cock in your ass?"

He scoffs. "Why does that matter?"

"You know why."

His expression softens with embarrassment. "It's been a while," he admits.

As I thought.

"I'll go easy on you then." I let go of his balls and he sighs with relief. "You will be panting my name by the end of the night."

CHAPTER EIGHT
HOOK

Bloody hell, what am I doing?

The voice of Commander Hook is trying desperately to get in.

Poor form.

Poor form.

Am I sober? Am I thinking straight?

I feel sober. More so than I've ever felt before, but I must be losing my fucking mind to be trailing after the Crocodile and his cloud of smoke like a lost puppy dog.

His shoulders are level as he strolls through the streets a few paces ahead of me. Light from the lampposts casts a halo around his dark silhouette and even though he's in front of me, the details of his body stuck in shadow, I can't help but hunger for the sharp lines of him. Every jutting bone, every dimple of muscle, ever hard valley between his abs.

I want to touch him. Desperately. I've gone fucking mad.

And now I'm so hard, it hurts to walk.

Finding a pool of shadow, I reach down to readjust myself, tucking my cock into the thick leather of my belt.

When the roof of The Royal Suit appears in the distance, my heart beats harder and I quicken my pace, falling in step beside the Crocodile.

I can't look at him while we walk.

If I look at him, I'm afraid of what I'll see and what I might do when I see it.

He warned me there was no turning back.

I'm not afraid of walking away.

I'm afraid of the regret if I did.

I would always wonder what it might have been like, facing my greatest enemy, and then taking pleasure from him.

Oh who the fuck am I kidding?

I just fucking want him.

That's it.

Can a man not seek pleasure where it's freely given?

When we turn into the courtyard of the inn, I pull the keys from my pocket, the metal clanking in the deepening night.

The Crocodile says nothing but breaks open a peanut fished from his trousers and tosses the nut in his mouth as I fumble with the lock.

My stomach tilts, adrenaline rushing through my veins.

I get the bolt unlocked. There is a single lantern glowing from the hook by the door. It's enough light to see by and I toss the keys onto the table, then reach for the bottle of rum.

I pour. I drink. I wince at the burn.

The Crocodile shuts the door with the sole of his boot.

He is no longer eating his peanuts, no longer smoking his cigarettes.

He is staring at me with an intensity that could scald.

I swallow hard.

"You're steering this ship, Captain," he says with a teasing lilt to his voice. "Tell me where you want me."

He's giving me control?

No, this is just part of the game.

I lick my lips, pour another drink, toss it back.

When the liquor warms the chill creeping up my spine, I say, "I want to fuck your arrogant fucking face."

He grins at me, all sharp teeth, and spreads out his arms, then slowly sinks to his knees on the rag rug beside the bed.

The faucet drips behind me and outside the room, a breeze rattles the branches of an old oak tree.

What am I to do with the Crocodile now that I have him?

Maybe I don't know what I'm getting into.

Maybe I am in way over my head.

"Well?" he coaxes.

He and I both know this is a direct answer to his earlier goading about blowjobs.

...a man is never more vulnerable than he is when his cock is in someone's mouth.

This is my way of saying I'm not afraid.

Even though my heart is racing. Even though I don't know where to begin, where to end, and if I might lose myself somewhere in the middle.

I set the empty glass down and cross the room to him.

My breath catches in my throat like a gale wind caught in an alley. Just circling uselessly, over and over again.

Roc looks up at me from his place on the floor and even though it's a position of submission, neither of us is foolish enough to think he is submitting to me.

The Crocodile is just playing to see how far I'll go.

Taking a deep breath through my nose, I unzip my pants, then undo the button. I'm already straining against my underwear and the Crocodile doesn't miss it.

"Show me," he demands. "Show me the cock Wendy Darling chose over mine."

I catch the edge of his jealousy, but don't hesitate.

I reach in around the waistband, fisting myself and a needy little sigh comes out of my throat before I can stop it. The Crocodile smiles.

My heart lurches in my chest.

When I pull myself out to the flickering lantern light, the Crocodile drags the tip of his tongue over his teeth.

There's no turning back.

I won't show him any fear.

This is my revenge, not his.

I stroke myself and my cock swells in my fist.

The Crocodile's nostrils flare when I'm fully engorged, when the head of my dick glistens with pre-cum.

"Get the fuck over here, Captain," he demands and closes the last foot between us by yanking me close by the hip of my trousers.

Suddenly I'm inside of him, enveloped in the wet, hot heat of his mouth.

"Bloody...hell," I gasp out, all of the excitement and pleasure and exhilaration fizzing in my veins, ready to pop.

He controls me by the hips, his grip on me tight, bruising, while his mouth glides over me, tongue swirling around my cock.

I hang my head back, squeeze my eyes shut.

Fuck.

Fuck.

I can't think straight.

Fucking hell he's good.

He increases the tempo, sucking harder. I'm panting now and I can't hide the desire, the desperate need for more of him. I can't hide anything from the Crocodile when my dick is in his mouth.

I thread my fingers through the coarse waves of his dark hair, taking charge. I thrust deep, teeth gritted, but he doesn't choke on me. Of course, the Crocodile would be unruffled by getting railed in the face. He knows just how to angle, to take every fucking inch of me.

I can't stop. I don't want to stop. It's like he's worshipping me. Me. Of all people. I feel like I'm the king of the fucking world.

And when he takes my balls in hand, squeezes just enough to be painful, the pressure makes me see stars.

I'm going to nut in his fucking mouth. My mortal enemy. And he's going to take it because I'm going to make him.

I huff out and I make the mistake of glancing down at him and it's this, the sight of him, one of the most dangerous men in the Seven Isles, on his knees for me, it's this that undoes me. How eager I am to fill him up, how willing he is to take me.

The orgasm comes out of nowhere, the heat of the pleasure matching the tight heat of his mouth as I fill him with cum.

A full body shake runs through me and my hips hitch forward, burying myself to the back of his throat.

The Crocodile doesn't complain. In fact, his eyes are bright and searching as if this is the most amusing thing he's ever endured.

I try pulling back, but he locks me in place another

second longer, taking the last drop of me, his soft tongue swirling over my slit.

A whetted breath huffs out of me.

When I finally stumble back, my cock sticky with cum and his spit, he smiles at me, his lips glistening as he climbs to his full height. There is a bead of cum on the corner of his mouth and using the pad of his thumb, he swipes it away, then sucks it off like it's the most delicious thing he's ever tasted.

I wish I had a ship railing to hold on to because I feel like I'm about to spill over the edge.

Instead I backpedal until I meet the wall.

Pain sings across my stomach, driving away the ecstasy.

"Captain," he says.

I blink several times. "What?"

"You're bleeding again."

I look down and see fresh blood seeping through his makeshift bandage.

"Bloody hell," I breathe out and then the room tilts and I finally spill over.

CHAPTER NINE
ROC

I catch the Captain before he hits the floor. He's dead weight in my arms and I adjust my stance to keep us both upright.

"Give me a warning next time," I tell him, scooping him into my arms. He's lighter than I would have expected. More bone than muscle.

I could break him easily, without thinking.

Crossing the room, I set him on the bed, the old springs creaking with his added weight. I rearrange him to get a better look at his wounds, tearing off his shirt, then the bandage. The cut is weeping again, but it's not red. Now, in the light, I realize he's bleeding black.

Well that's interesting.

I try to think back to the moment I took his hand. Did he bleed red then? The lighting had been dim, the moment full of chaos and triumph and glee. I hadn't paid attention.

I scan the Captain's face for any sign of life, but he's still out cold.

I dip a hand into my pocket and pull out a peanut,

crushing into its shell as I think absently about what secrets the Captain might be hiding.

It can't be coincidence, the fact he bleeds black and he's terrified of the sight of his own blood.

"Don't move," I tell his unconscious body and head over to the tavern.

At this late hour, the place is nearly empty. I find the innkeeper wiping down tables.

"We're closed," she calls before she looks up. "Oh. It's you."

"It's me." I go behind the counter and pour myself a glass of fairy wine. The sweetness blooms on my tongue, mixing well with the saltiness of the Captain's cum. "I need a needle and thread and some strips of cloth if you have it," I tell Mills.

She watches me with the kind of cautious distance that only someone familiar with my kind would.

"If you've got some mending that needs doing, you can leave the garments with me and—"

"Not that kind of mending."

She straightens, the wet rag hanging from her grasp. "I see. Your friend? The captain?"

I nod, a desperate yank making me cranky. "I haven't got all night."

"Of course. Sorry Jab—"

I cut her off. "No one knows me by that name here. Never speak it."

The blush that hits her cheeks spreads down her neck, pooling at her cleavage. "I...I didn't mean..."

"Fetch it now, Mills, before I lose my patience."

She tosses the rag into a nearby bucket and dirty water sloshes over the rim. She hurries through a swinging door into the back.

I light a cigarette, inhale deeply, the smoke swirling in my lungs.

There's the sound of hands rifling through drawers in back. I pace the bar, the cigarette caught between my knuckles.

My head is starting to hurt, but I'm not sure why.

I don't get hangovers. I don't get headaches.

Mills returns with a small tin of thread, several different-sized needles, a ball of jagged strips of cloth, and a glass jar of red salve. "Put the salve on after you've stitched him up."

"Magic or nature?" I ask her.

"Magic."

"What kind?"

She taps at the heart stitched over her chest. The Red Suit Caste. It speaks to how distracted I've been that I didn't notice it before.

But it begs the question—what is she doing so far from home?

Not my problem. Not my concern.

"Thank you." I hand over one of my bars of fairy gold. Her eyes get big, but she doesn't return it.

"Don't disturb us," I tell her.

She gives me a quick nod before I duck out the back door.

I finish the cigarette and toss the butt into a nearby tumbler of rum. The lit end sizzles and goes dark.

At the table, I set out the items Mills gave me and find the right sized needle. I'm no stranger to mending wounds. Vane and I would stitch each other up more often than I'd like to admit. Being what we are, we healed quickly, but closing the wound shortened the time by half and we were always short on time in the Darkland Umbrage.

Tick-tock. Tick-tock.

It seems so long ago now, when my little brother and I ruled the dark side of the city.

Sometimes I think about going back just to see how much it's changed.

Thinking about it has my attention wandering to the rock hanging from my neck. A gift from my little brother that still pulses with warmth. The Darkland Dark Shadow. There is no gift that holds more value or power than this.

If I returned to my home island, I could rule it if I took on the power of the shadow. And yet here I am, on an island not my own, with a man who hates me as much as desires me, looking for a woman who rejected me. And for what? To prove a point? To who?

I pull the chair over to the bedside and set the tin on the table, the needle and thread inside.

Leaning over, I slap the Captain on the face and he lurches upright.

"Don't look down," I tell him.

He nearly does, until he remembers, until he sees the seriousness on my face.

"I'm going to stitch you up." I flick my lighter to flame and hold the needle to the heat. "You're going to shut the fuck up and let me do it. Aye, Captain?"

He licks his lips and drops back to the pillows. He's pale and sweaty. "Aye," he says, his voice a husky drawl.

I clean the wound first with a clean cloth and splash of rum and the Captain hisses from the sting.

The cloth comes away black. I toss it to the floor, out of view.

I prep the needle, running thread through the eye, tying off the end into a neat little knot.

"Why do you hate the sight of your own blood?" I ask him, pinching his wound between thumb and forefinger, making him wince.

"It's a long story."

"Then shorten it."

I pierce his flesh and he grits his teeth, hands balled into the sheets.

"My father," he says on a rush of air when the needle clears his flesh. "He caught me..." He swallows and takes a breath. "He caught me with a servant. He said I was an embarrassment, that I was a stain on the name Hook for cavorting with the help."

I run back through and he pauses, inhaling, holding it in until I close up another stitch.

"Afterward, he took me to a woman. We called her the Witch in the Woods. She knew magic and practiced it too at a time when most people couldn't grow herbs without being hung for it. But Commander William H. Hook was fine with using it if it solved him a problem."

The Captain relaxes when another stitch is finished. I stall, giving him a break.

"He told the witch to show me my sins. I don't remember much of what happened after that. She cut me, then gave me a tea that tasted awful and I remember waking up at home, in my own bed. I thought it had been a dream and I forgot about it for a time. Until I displeased my father again. And he cut me across the face and showed me my reflection."

He closes his eyes, tension pressing into the fine lines. "I was bleeding black. I thought it was the plague." He laughs at the ridiculousness. "He told me, 'Your sins will always leave a stain, boy. Can you do nothing right? Poor form. *Poor form, indeed.*'"

When his eyes turn glassy with the memory, I run the needle through again and he curses, flinching back.

"So you bleed black when you've done something wrong. Is that it?" I ask him.

He exhales, long and through his nose. "That's it, yes."

"Have you ever cut yourself when you've done something good?" I run the last stitch through and tie it off, biting through the thread to shorten it. "It would be interesting, wouldn't it? To see what color you would bleed."

His eyes catch mine. He gives me no words, but I still hear them.

He's never done something he would consider good. He's never done anything he believes his father would approve of.

He and I have that in common.

My father was disappointed in me the moment I was born. I still bear that reminder in my true name.

Setting the needle aside, I uncap the glass jar containing the crimson salve. It smells sweet like cinnamon and anise, but I think that's just an illusion. Magical salves usually smell like sulphuric bogs.

Mills is clearly more powerful than I'd given her credit for.

Dipping my fingers inside, I pull out a generous heaping of the salve and then cake it onto the wound.

The Captain grunts again. "What is that?"

"It'll help stave off infection."

When the wound is sufficiently covered, I waggle my fingers at him. "Get up."

With a heavy sigh, he swings his legs over the side of the bed, moving slowly, avoiding looking down at the wound. He's done bleeding but perhaps he's being cautious.

I take a length of the clean cloth and wrap it around his torso, covering the wound. We are inches apart so it's easy to hear the shift in his breathing, the way the air catches in his throat. I just sucked him off but he's still apprehensive around me. As if my teeth close to his neck is somehow more dangerous than my teeth raking over his cock.

When the wound is properly dressed, I order him back down and he grimaces with pain as he readjusts on the mattress, trying to get the pillow between him and the headboard. I help him just to end his and my misery.

"No sudden movements," I warn him. "Or you'll risk ripping the stitches."

"I know," he growls.

I pour him a glass of rum. He takes it happily and downs it quickly.

He holds the empty glass in hand, balancing the bottom on the thin quilt where it dips down between his thighs.

Doubt creeps into the soft planes of his face like an afternoon shadow stretching out with the night.

He is wondering if what he's done has somehow changed him just as I'd promised.

I am not often at a loss for words, but I have none to offer him now, none that would be comforting.

I devour. I do not coddle.

"Now what?" he dares to ask me.

I collapse into the chair beside the table.

"Now you rest."

"But Wendy—"

"She's been here for a very long time. A few more hours won't hurt."

His shoulders relax and he sinks further into the pillow. "Have you thought about what you'll say to her when you see her for the first time?"

"Not really," I admit. "Have you?"

He nods to himself. "'*I'm sorry.*'"

I slouch in the chair and cross my legs at the ankle. "If she is anything like the girl we knew last, she will use your apology like a wild card, pulling it out of her sleeve when she needs it most."

Wendy Darling was never as innocent as she pretended to be. It's what I liked most about her.

The Captain sets the empty glass on the bedside table. "What if she tells us to go get fucked?"

I can tell he means it to be a joke, but even I, the Devourer of Men, know the low tenor of worry.

"What if she does? I'm sure we could entertain ourselves easily enough."

His nostrils flare, imagining all the things we could get up to, but then he remembers himself, remembers who we are and asks, "What are we doing, Roc?"

It's the first time I've ever heard him call me by my name. Or at least the name he knows.

"What do you mean?" I ask, because there is nothing I desire more than making a man uncomfortable.

He gives me a withering look. "Don't be so difficult."

"Would you rather I be easy?"

He rolls his eyes.

I sigh. "What are we doing, Captain?" I repeat. "We are having fun. Nothing more. Nothing less."

When I see the hurt on his face, I nearly take it back. But I can't really have pirate captains falling for me, now can I?

Especially one as handsome as Captain Hook.

He is like a delicate Pleasureland dessert. Meant to be desired. Meant to make a man a glutton. More and more and more. Just like fairy wine, very rarely can you stop with just one.

He is elegant and refined like a latticed pastry. Tempting and sharp like a lemon tart.

If I'm not careful, I might find myself craving the taste of the Captain on the back of my tongue.

More and more and more.

I stand up. The Captain follows my movements and the worry I heard earlier is now reflected in his eyes and the pinch between his dark brows. "Where are you going?"

"For a walk," I tell him and pull out my pocket watch, checking the time. "I need a bite."

Color blooms across his cheeks, but there is a war brewing in his gaze. If there are things he wants to say, he chooses not to say them.

I'm still a few hours off from needing blood to stave off the beast taking over, but if I stay here any longer, I may be sinking my teeth into the Captain.

And that we can't have.

It wouldn't be good for either one of us.

"Don't get into too much trouble," he tells me.

I smile at him with all my teeth. "But Captain, it's what I'm good at."

CHAPTER TEN

HOOK

The silence blooms in the Crocodile's absence.

There is only the sound of my ragged breathing and the dripping of the washroom faucet.

I lay back into the pillows, close my eyes, and try to drift, but I can smell him everywhere.

In the air. On the bed. On my skin.

I can't stop replaying the scene in my head.

The Crocodile on his knees. My cock in his mouth.

It takes no more than that to be painfully, obscenely rock hard.

Bloody hell.

Gingerly, I swing my legs over the side of the bed and heft myself up trying to keep my torso straight so as not to rip the stitches.

Once on my feet, I shuffle over to the table, my elbow tight against my side trying to keep myself together.

Please don't start bleeding again.

That's just what I need, the Crocodile returning to find me splayed out on the floor having fainted again at the sight of my own blood.

What an embarrassment.

I pour a drink and sling it back, but it does nothing to soothe my frayed nerves or the unsettled feeling in my gut.

I gave in to temptation and I'm not sure how I feel about it or how the Crocodile might use it against me.

Shame burns through my blood.

I should have known better.

I should have been stronger.

I knock back another shot and the alcohol finally hits, buzzing through my body, unknotting some of the tension in my gut and the dread in my heart.

There is only one reason I came to Everland and it isn't to have an illicit affair with my immortal enemy.

It takes every ounce of strength I have to ease myself back into the bed. Once I'm lying flat on my back, I give in to the fuzzy warmth of the liquor and the relief I feel at having made it back to the mattress without fainting.

Sleep, I tell myself.

Just for a few hours.

And when I wake, perhaps all of this will be forgotten and I can move on with my mission so I can finally put the Crocodile behind me.

I should have known it wouldn't be that easy.

I wake to Roc kicking the bed. "Get up," he shouts but in a whisper and I half rise.

"What the bloody hell are you doing?"

His hand is on my mouth in an instant and my breath puffs out around his fingers. There is an emotion on his face, not quite fear, but a second cousin of it. Apprehension maybe.

"I was followed," he tells me, removing his hand, then thrusting a shirt into my chest.

"Who?"

"Get dressed." He goes to the window and looks out. There is still darkness beyond the thin, bubbled glass so I must not have been out long. Thankfully some of the pain has ebbed in my side suggesting my body did the miracle of fast healing while I slept.

I don't heal like Peter Pan or his Lost Boys, or like Roc. But I'm not as disadvantaged as a mortal. It's been that way ever since I was a young man.

I slip the shirt on over my head, then get up and tuck it into my trousers, secure my belt back into place.

"Who followed you?"

The Crocodile's gaze is still on the courtyard beyond our room.

"I'm not sure. And I'm still trying to decide if we should allow them to catch us."

"*What*? Why would we want that?"

He doesn't answer me so I sit on the edge of the bed to buckle up my boots. This is one of the biggest things that changed when Peter Pan and the Crocodile took my hand. I could no longer tie boots with a hook. It was much easier to buckle and snap.

Inevitably, when I think about that night, the phantom pain comes back and for a second, my mind plays tricks on me making me think the hand is still there, that I can flex my fingers.

"Probably best if we run," the Crocodile decides and crosses the room to me. "Do you have everything of importance?"

I didn't pack much. I scan the room and find only my

bottle of rum, some loose coinage. I think my comb might be in the washroom along with the straight razor I used to shave my face clean when I landed here.

"I'm good," I tell him and he nods.

"We climb out the back window."

"You still haven't told me who we're running from."

He yanks the entire curtain and rod off the wall with little care and tosses it aside. The back window looks out on an uncut hedge and some briar bushes. It's narrower, and shorter, than the front windows. Climbing through won't be easy.

"Up you go," he orders me.

"You first."

He rolls his eyes at me. "I have two hands. I can pull myself through." He threads his fingers together creating a step for me. "Hurry, Captain."

I am distantly aware of the fact that the Crocodile can hear much farther than I can and must know better than I do just how much time we have. And yet I look down at his cupped hands and the tension around his eyes and decide it's the perfect time to be difficult.

"What if this is some kind of ploy to get me out of my room and lock the door behind me? So I have to sleep in the bushes?"

His brow furrows. "I assure you, Captain, I wouldn't waste my time on ploys."

He says the word like it's a child's game, like it's beneath him.

"You have about five seconds," he tells me.

"Five seconds?!"

"One."

I look from him to the front door and back to him.

"Two."

I'm still barely awake, barely thinking straight.

"Three."

"Christ," I say and plant my boot in his hands.

"Four."

"I'm going. I'm going!"

I place my hand and hook on his shoulder, braced for him to haul me up.

The front door bursts open, splintered right down the middle by a hand-carved battering ram with a roaring lion's head on the front end.

"You dragged your feet too long, Captain," the Crocodile mutters to me, unlinking his hands and dropping my foot back to the floor.

Several men spill in.

It is immediately clear who they are — they're wearing the uniform of the royal guards. Navy blue pants and jacket with royal blue epaulets and a crest embroidered on the left chest in matching royal blue and gold. The roaring lion's head. The mark of the Grimmaldi family.

"On your knees!" the stout man in front bellows.

I look over at the Crocodile. "What did you do?"

"Me? Nothing." He smiles at me like he might be lying.

"On your knees. Now!"

"I must apologize for this beast," I say. "He is neither friend nor companion. Whatever he has done, I have no part—"

The stout man waggles a finger and a lanky man behind him comes around and punches me right in the nose.

"What the bloody hell?!" I stumble back and then sink to my knees, covering my nose just in case there is blood.

Thankfully I seem unharmed save for the ringing in my ears and the blurring of my vision.

"Apprehend them," someone proclaims and within seconds, I'm handcuffed and yanked from the room by the Everland Royal Guard.

CHAPTER ELEVEN
ROC

WE'RE TOSSED INTO A CARRIAGE WITH BARS ON THE DOORS AND NO windows to see out. Our handcuffs are linked through a chain in either wall. The Captain is positioned on the bench across from me, but the carriage is so small and so narrow that he has to close his legs to fit between mine.

The door is unceremoniously slammed shut, the bolt locked into place.

Once the horses are coaxed into action, the wagon lurches forward.

The Captain lowers his voice to a disgruntled whisper and says, "What the bloody hell did you do while I was sleeping?!"

Truth be told, I didn't do much of anything except escape for some air and a little blood. I paid the dockhand a duket to open his veins for me. It's more than I give most people. He didn't fuss about it, even when I drank a little too much.

It was on my way back to the inn that I realized I was being watched, and then followed.

By then it was too late. They clearly knew who I was and where I was staying.

The question is, why does the royal guard care enough to apprehend me?

I dine with royalty. I'm not typically seized by them. I'm too handsome and charming for that.

"I think the question you should be asking instead is, 'What do we do now?'"

"No!" He lunges forward as if to wring my neck, but the chains catch him and he falls back to the bench. "If I knew what you did, I would know how to assure them I had no part in it."

"Do you really wish to be free of me so soon?" I'm poking fun at him, but I'm still curious about the answer.

He huffs and falls back against the carriage wall. About every twenty feet or so, the light from the next streetlamp washes across his face through the barred door and I'm given a glance of the sharp lines of anxiety in the space between his brows.

"No need to worry, Captain." I smile at him. Even in the dark, I know my teeth will show bright. "I've been in more precarious situations than this."

"We've been arrested."

"Yes."

"By the royal guard."

"Yes."

"I think this is one of the most precarious situations two men can find themselves in."

I smile wider. "Well not *thee* most."

We're in a spot of darkness, traveling in the dead space between two lampposts. He is shrouded in shadow, but I imagine the redness pooling in his face. I imagine him recalling the precarious situation his dick was in just a few hours ago.

"Will you stop?" he says.

"Do I have to?"

He huffs again but says nothing more, and I can't quite tell if he's sick of me or desperate for more.

Sometimes they are very close to the same thing.

The carriage makes its way around Avis, then pauses at a guard station at the castle's curtain wall. There is a conversation between guards, then a lantern raised to our barred door to verify its occupants.

I wave hello.

The Captain raises his hand to shield his eyes from the light. His chain rattles.

"What's with the hook?" the new guard asks. "You should have seized all weapons." The light from his lantern glazes his sweaty face.

The other guard, the one who struck the Captain back at the inn and who will pay for it someday soon, says, "Peter Pan stole his hand. The hook is a replacement for it."

"Ahh yes." The sweaty man presses his face to the bars to peer in at us. "The infamous Captain Hook, is it?"

"Wait," I say across the carriage. "You're Captain Hook?"

He screws up his face at me. "What are you doing?"

"I had no idea!" I slide down the bench and get as close to the doors as I can. "You have to get me out of here. He's diabolical, I hear. Pursued Peter Pan with violence and tenacity the likes of which we've never seen."

The sweaty guard frowns. "I *have* heard he's a ruthless pirate."

"Yes!" I shout. "He'll kill me just for sport, I bet."

"Will you knock it off?" the Captain says through gritted teeth.

"Please, sir. I barely know this man. I thought he was hiring me for some cleaning. I'm poor. Just a beggar, you see."

"That true?" the glazed pastry asks the other guard.

"Don't let him fool you," the soon-to-be-dead man says. "That one right there? That's the Crocodile. The Devourer of Men."

The sweaty pastry widens his eyes and lurches back. He drops the lantern and the glass shatters, the flame snuffing out.

The other guards laugh at his expense and he sputters in counter. "I didn't recognize him! I didn't know."

The man who punched the Captain gives the embarrassed guard a pat on the shoulder. "Fair not, Basker. You're right to be afraid. He's more dangerous than the pirate."

"Christ," the Captain mutters.

"Sorry." I bump his knee with mine and wink at him. "Looks like I'm more infamous than you."

"Will this night never end?"

"If you're lucky, it won't."

He rests his head against the carriage wall and closes his eyes. "What was I thinking, teaming up with you?"

The guards disappear from the barred doors and continue their cajoling of Basker before the gate is finally opened and the horses ushered forward.

"Where we taking them?" one of the guards asks.

"Straight to the queen," the sweaty man answers.

The Captain sits upright.

I tilt my head, ear toward the barred door.

"Never transferred a prisoner straight to the court," Basker says.

The carriage veers left away from the castle's main entrance. We're taken around back to an unmarked door tucked into a thick stone wall.

Just over the curtain wall, the sun is begging to break free of the night.

I should be sleeping but I'm high on blood, cum, and curiosity.

I'm not familiar with the queen of Everland. I had heard their court was influenced by dark witches.

I have faced two such witches in my days. The first one nearly killed me. The second conned me out of my pants, then my shirt, and then convinced me I was a parrot. I spent months craving crackers instead of peanuts.

I don't much relish the idea of facing another.

The carriage door is unlocked. The dead man appears and gives me a stern warning not to get any ideas about escaping. I nod solemnly. Why would I escape when a mystery is so close at hand?

Plus, it'll be easier to kill him if I play the part of a dutiful prisoner.

The Captain is unlatched first. He ducks when he's escorted out and the wagon jostles when he hops down.

I'm next. My heart beats a little harder, seeing the thumping vein in the guard's neck. I could take him now. But with several other guards standing by, I would have to be quick and there's no retribution in a swift death.

"When I kill you," I tell him as my chain hits the carriage floor, "I will make it violent."

His eyes narrow. "What did you say?"

I used the ancient language. The language of the Bone Society.

The language of monsters.

I wink at him. "It's an old saying. It translates to, 'Thank you, kind sir.'"

Close enough.

We are taken through the unmarked door. It opens onto a stone hallway just wide enough for one man, elbows tucked into his sides. Flaming sconces hang from the wall, and shadows dance as we descend further into the palace.

When we emerge, our boots go silent on plush red carpeting.

We're getting closer now.

The stone wall gives way to more and more windows and the sharp golden rays of new sunlight pour in through the colorful stained glass.

"This way," the guard says and gestures for us to turn right down an arched hallway.

"If we're to see the queen," I ask as I pass, "do we really need the handcuffs?"

"I'd say you need more than handcuffs, but I'm not in charge."

"I do love a good bondage party."

He gives me a shove and I rattle forward.

When we enter our final destination, there is a red carpet running from the doorway up to a dais where a dainty throne sits empty.

The queen's receiving room.

There are no windows here. No second floor gallery. Barely any furniture.

This is not a room where the queen entertains.

As we are pushed down the carpet, I spot a demure silhouette waiting in the shadows of the dais. It's done up like a stage, with heavy brocade drapes tied off at each side casting deep shadows to the recess.

Once we've reached the five stone steps that lead up to

the dais, we are yanked to a standstill, then shoved to our knees.

"The night has officially ended, Captain, but I suspect the fun has only begun."

"Will you shut up?"

"Quiet!" Her voice rings out with authority, but it is not overwhelmed by age. It's clear and steady.

My eyesight is better than a mortal's, but I think she's purposefully obscured herself to make it harder for me to see.

And my second bout of apprehension slithers in.

If she's purposefully hiding from me, then she knows what I am. Not just my reputation. But that I'm not mortal. Not human.

Something else.

And there are so few people who know the *else*.

"Captain," I say.

"Shhh," he says back.

"Captain, I think—"

"Silence!" she yells and the guard whacks me with his wooden baton.

The force of the hit vibrates through my skull and down my spine.

That guard is double dead now.

The heels of her shoes clack loudly on the stone and then go abruptly silent when she hits the red carpet.

It's jarring, the loudness, then the silence and I frown against the sensory unease.

That is until she's free of the shadows. Until my eyes take her in.

The frown turns into gaping. I don't gape. Not often. Sometimes maybe. Sometimes when I see something pretty I like and want to fuck or bite.

Once upon a time, I wanted all from her. I wanted to fucking drown in her. I wanted her to make me forget.

"When the queen asks for silence, you obey," she says.

The Captain's mouth drops open too and he breaks her rule within seconds of her declaring it.

"Wendy Darling," he says. "You're alive."

CHAPTER TWELVE
WENDY

THEY'RE HERE.

They're fucking here.

I clasp my hands behind my back to hide my shaking, but I'm not sure I can hide my unease from Roc. Nothing ever escaped him.

I straighten my shoulders as Theo's gaze shifts to me. Theo is the Captain of the Royal Guard and I tasked him with this mission. There are only two people in this entire god forsaken court whom I trust: Theo and Asha. And Asha told me not to go through with this.

Looking at them now, the two men I once desired more than anything, I know Asha was right.

This was a mistake.

But I'm in too deep and now I must dig my way out.

When word came back to me that two men were in town asking for me by my old name, my first thought was Peter Pan, maybe one of the Lost Boys.

When Asha told me it was Roc and James, that not only were they both looking for me, but that they seemed to be working together, I had to see it for myself.

They were mortal enemies once. Roc took James's hand as punishment for touching me.

Now they are kneeling side by side, shoulders practically touching.

I think I have miscalculated.

All of it.

Them.

Me.

How risky it would be to bring them here in front of the Royal Guard.

Theo is my ally, but for how long? One wrong move and he'll switch sides. I know he will. Theo is only out for Theo and right now I've given him the impression that should he remain by my side, I will marry him and make him king.

Even he must know that's a shaky promise. After all, I married into the royal family, I was not born into it, and worse, I started out as their prisoner.

It's a miracle I got to this point.

And it's that miracle that is now threatening to have me beheaded.

I am on shaky ground. And Roc and James reappearing is the last thing I need.

If Hally catches wind that men from my old life have resurfaced...

I swallow as a lump forms in my throat.

I have to get them out of here. Out of Everland.

"Wendy Darling is dead," I tell them. "You would do well to keep that name off your tongue. Do you understand?"

James sputters.

Roc elbows him.

James gives him a sharp look but goes quiet.

"Of course, we understand, Your Majesty," Roc says and gives me a slight bow of his head.

There are so many questions I have.

What has changed? Are they friends now? And where is Peter Pan? The Lost Boys? And what of the Darling women?

What of my baby?

Once I was made Queen of Everland, the doorways to the Seven Isles opened for me and any information I wanted, I could have had.

But I didn't ask. I was too afraid of what the answers might be.

Did Smee make it back to the mortal realm with my daughter? Was she able to hide her? Did the tyranny of the Peter Pan curse end with me?

I'm so close to asking them now, that I have to bite my tongue to stop myself. Theo will not like me looking back — it would sow doubt.

But something changed if Roc and James are here.

I both want to know and don't want to know.

I will not dig up old graves.

They left me here to die, to fend for myself. I must never forget that.

I look to Theo. "Escort them to the docks. They are not allowed back on Everland soil."

"Yes, Your Majesty," he says.

"And be quick about it, Theo," I add unable to hide the urgency in my voice.

"Of course." Theo tips his head in acknowledgment.

What I haven't said is, *Make sure Hally doesn't see them.*

"Good day then," I turn away, my heart storming up my throat.

"Wait!" James yells. "That can't be...Wendy, I mean, *Your Majesty*—we've come all this way..."

But I don't want to know why they're here. It doesn't matter.

I slip into the shadows of the dais, then through a hidden door tucked behind the heavy drapes. When I'm safely inside the Queen's Tunnel, I run. I run as fast as I can and as far as I can and try to pretend this has changed nothing when it's changed absolutely everything.

CHAPTER THIRTEEN
HOOK

SHE IS MORE BEAUTIFUL THAN I REMEMBERED.

Though she has left us, the image of her in regal dress and a queen's diamond crown is seared into the space behind my eyes.

Wendy Darling is alive and she's the queen of Everland?

No longer is she the young, innocent Darling girl snatched up by Peter Pan and whisked away to Neverland.

She is a woman.

A survivor.

A fucking queen.

Her face has sharpened, her cheeks a little hollower, her eyes dark and haunted. She may have matured, but she hasn't aged by much. Not like she should have with all the time that's passed.

How did she do it? How has time not touched her? Is it some kind of magic?

The dockmaster said something about the court being overrun by witches.

The guard pushes us toward the door.

I look over at Roc. How is he taking this so well? Why isn't he demanding she return? Demanding answers?

He looks calm as can be.

We're ushered out of the room and down the same hall and down the same narrow tunnel until we emerge in the early daylight.

"These still necessary?" Roc asks. "Theo was it? We really mean no harm. Clearly, we've made an innocent mistake."

The guard grumbles to himself, then fetches a key from his pocket. He undoes my cuffs first, then Roc's.

"This way," Theo says and gestures with his hand, indicating we should follow the stone path back to the gated entrance.

We take the lead. Roc lights a cigarette. He says nothing, just follows the stones beneath our feet.

What is wrong with him?

I want him to be ruffled.

I want him to join me in this unyielding sense of despondency.

Wendy Darling is alive and yet she looked at us like we were an inconvenience. A bad memory. One she wanted to wipe the slate clean of.

And she's the queen?

How the bloody hell did that happen?

I have so many questions.

When we reach the gate, Theo instructs the guards to open it. The chain system clangs to life and the iron gate slowly lifts.

Are we really going to walk through that gate and never look back?

I can't.

I can't do that.

"Roc," I start, but he immediately cants his head, narrows his eyes, silences me with a look that only he can wield.

"You both would do well to keep your fucking mouths shut," Theo says.

Roc doesn't break our stare for several long seconds and while his expression is blank, his only movement that of the cigarette at his lips, I have come to know that tension in his body.

It is the tension of an ocean right before a storm.

He's going to kill this man.

Maybe not right this second, but someday, maybe soon.

"Don't worry, Theo," Roc finally says and pulls the cigarette away. "We heard the queen. We will play the role of dutiful little boys."

Theo's mouth presses into a thin line. He doesn't like us and it begs the question: what is his relationship with the queen? I would place my money on it being more than just guard and queen.

And thinking about him on top of her makes me want to drag my hook across his gut and let his insides spill out.

I may be fighting Roc for the opportunity to kill him.

"Good," Theo says and nods us forward. "Let's make haste before—"

"Theo? Is that you?"

The lilting posh accent sounds from our left and I catch the imperceptible wince on Theo's face.

Roc and I turn at once and spot a man making his way to us.

I don't recognize his face, but I know immediately who he is.

He's wearing the Grimmaldi crest, the Grimmaldi

signet ring, and the oversized gold chain, with interlocking links, known as the Collar of Ember.

Only the Crown Prince, the Heir Apparent, would wear that particular collar.

"Your Highness." Theo gives a shallow bow, his hands clasped behind his back. "Good morning. You're up and about early."

The Crown Prince stops, keeping several feet between us. His gaze rakes over me and Roc with an interest that is penetrating enough to make me cringe.

"I heard our dear queen had visitors today and I couldn't pass up the chance to meet them."

"Ahh," Theo answers, like he didn't already know why the prince was on the castle grounds at the crack of dawn.

Some of the answers I had so desired are starting to reveal themselves.

There is nothing in the prince's face that would connect him to Wendy, so she must be his stepmother. And of course the Crown Prince would hold a grudge against the woman on the throne who is not his mother.

The prince does not like the queen and he thinks he can use us against her.

"And you are?" the prince asks, giving me a pointed look.

"Captain James Hook," I answer distantly.

The prince glances at Roc.

Roc's expression is unreadable. He says nothing.

"This is the Crocodile," Theo answers for him.

The prince might want to pretend he's the one who holds all the power in this exchange, but none of us miss the step back that he takes once he finds out who Roc is.

There is something intoxicating about being Roc's traveling companion and watching how people react to him.

I get to stand beside him, almost his equal, no longer his enemy, and no longer afraid of him. Well, *mostly* unafraid.

I survived having my cock in his mouth so I feel like we are almost equals.

I very much doubt the prince would agree to be alone in the same room with Roc, and certainly not with his dick in his mouth.

"I've heard of you," the prince says.

"Of course you have," Roc answers.

The prince laughs, but the sound is miffed.

"You know our venerated queen then?"

Roc takes one last hit of his cigarette, then places the butt on the end of his thumb, flicking it with his index finger. It arches through the air, raining sparks, before landing at the prince's feet.

Theo chokes on his own spit.

The Crown Prince looks down at the still smoking cigarette, his nostrils flaring.

"Theo," he says when he looks back up. "Any friend of the queen is a friend of the entire court. Show these fine men to a room in the guest wing. They'll join us tonight for supper."

"Your Highness, with all due respect—"

"*Now*, Theo." The prince turns. "I look forward to getting to know you better over a king's feast," he says as he walks away. "Theo, make sure our guests have the proper attire."

"Of course, Your Highness."

When the prince disappears around the castle wall, Theo grabs us both by the arm and yanks us toward the castle. "You idiots. You have no idea what you've done, have you?"

I yank out of the guard's grip, but Roc lets himself be steered which I think must be one of the most sinister things he's ever done.

Theo must have a death wish to be manhandling a voracious beast.

"I'm not sure what you're referring to," Roc says. "But we've just been invited to dinner by the prince. I'd say we've done something very right."

Theo snorts and grabs me again. "You've endangered the queen by showing your faces here. She will not be happy."

Roc hangs his head back so he can look at me over Theo's shoulders. He gives me a wink.

I don't know what that's supposed to mean, but with him, it certainly can't be good.

"Come on," Theo says. "Looks like you're staying at the castle tonight. Good luck making it till morning."

"That sounds like a challenge," Roc says.

Theo snorts. "Consider it a warning."

CHAPTER FOURTEEN
WENDY

I FIND ASHA IN THE ROYAL LIBRARY, SEVERAL BOOKS OPEN ON THE worktable in front of her. There is an oil lamp glowing beside her, the light flickering over the thin vellum pages. She is deep in the recesses of the library where the early morning light streaming through the tall, arched windows has yet to penetrate the thick shadows.

Her dark hair is twisted and held back with a bone stick but several wispy strands have come loose and hang along her pale, oval face.

Asha isn't originally from Everland. She came to the island as a teenager, hired by the royal archives to translate ancient texts and complete the Everland Illuminated Collections. When that job was done, she joined the Royal Guard. Not only can she speak and write seven languages (three of which are dead) but she is also one of the most accomplished soldiers in the entire Everland army having earned herself the nickname Bonescar at the Battle of *Dri vo Dair* against the highlanders.

I consider myself incredibly lucky to call her my most trusted friend, my *best* friend.

When I come in, she doesn't look up and her pen continues to move across an empty sheet of vellum laid out beside her.

With the illuminated texts complete, she's taken to translating ancient Everland recipes for no other reason than it keeps her busy. She just recently completed the text for a biscuit recipe that the kitchen then tested. Best biscuits the castle has ever produced.

My mouth waters now just thinking of them. Perhaps with my breakfast if I can get word in early enough. I certainly deserve the treat after the morning I've had.

"Did you see them?" she asks, her eyes still on her work.

"Yes."

"And?"

I collapse in one of the leather side chairs, my queen's dress puffing up around me. It's pompous, this dress, with its delicate embroidery and jewel-encrusted collar and all of its many layers of tulle.

I feel stupid having chosen it in order to make a show for James and Roc.

The dress was meant to say, *I don't need you. Look at how far I've come.*

But the truth is, my crown is a lie and the dress is like a masquerade mask that does not fit.

Asha finally looks up. When she sees the expression on my face, she sets her pen in the brass holder, folds her hands over her middle. Her fingers are stained with ink but the bright red tattoos that cover her hands break through anyway.

The tattoos are in the language of her people, the Northern Winterlanders who live in the mountains and make their life among the windroot trees and crisp glacier lakes.

When I ask her why she doesn't return home she tells me only that her home no longer exists.

I've never pressed. I know exactly what that feels like.

"They've devastated you," she surmises.

I clamp my teeth tight against one another trying not to cry.

The emotion catches me by surprise.

Asha clicks her tongue. She's always been able to read me easily, and she's never been one to mince words.

"Why have they come now?" My voice wobbles and I take a breath. "After all this time?"

"They've heard you're a queen. They've come hungry for a queen's gifts."

"No." I close my eyes and in the darkness behind my lids I see them both, Roc and James, more handsome than when I left them. More men than wily boys. They are opposite sides of the same coin, one heads, one tails. One handsome and desperately elegant, the other unassumingly dangerous, sharply beautiful.

"They were surprised," I say. "They didn't know who I had become. They wouldn't have been in the Merchant District asking for me if they'd known my title."

Asha shoves her chair back and comes over, taking the matching leather chair across from me. She sits forward, her elbows on her knees. Asha only dresses in the attire of a soldier—rough but sturdy trousers, close-fitting tunic, leather vest. But Asha could wear a beggar's cape and look like a princess.

She has that air about her—that she can make the most of anything, even scraps.

"What did you tell them?" she asks.

"I told them nothing, then sent them away."

She tilts her head, regarding me with the same scrutiny

she gives to ancient texts that must be unraveled and deciphered.

"But you wish you didn't have to."

I lick my lips. A breath catches in my throat. "I wish...I wish I could have spoken to them longer."

"And if you had, what would you have said?"

My chest grows tight and my usually steely facade crumbles, tears welling in my eyes. Asha is the only person I trust to see my vulnerability and never use it against me. But it's still painful to admit I have any.

"I would have said, '*How dare you abandon me.*'"

My chin trembles as the tears fill up my eyes.

Asha sits back and lets me have this moment of despair.

I swipe at my face as a few tears escape.

Any sign of emotion must be dealt with like a festering wound — you must rid yourself of all signs of it, first by purging its infection, then searing off the raw edges.

In a place like the Everland Court, there is no room for weakness.

When the moment is over, I look up at the library's vaulted ceiling, where the wrought iron chandeliers still flicker with candlelight, and blink back the last of the wetness in my eyes.

Turning to Asha, I sit upright and level my shoulders, pretend I didn't just break apart.

"You think they'll abide by your orders?" she asks. "Having come all this way for you?"

"I think they have little choice. I made Theo escort them to the docks."

Asha looks away, lost in thought.

"What is it?" I ask.

"I saw Hally earlier on my way to the library."

I lurch upright. "You didn't."

"He said he was headed to the healer for stomach pain, but now that I think about it..."

"What, Ash? Go on. Don't leave me hanging."

"When I left him, Hally headed in the opposite direction."

I'm on my feet in an instant.

"Wendy, *wait*."

But I can't. I can't wait.

There is no time to wait.

I'm out the door in an instant, my skirt bunched up in my hands. Asha is silent behind me, but I know she's following. She won't let me confront Hally alone. "Which way did he go?"

The library is on the third floor and I take the staircase down to the first landing, then turn the corner, down the next flight until I reach the mezzanine that sits in the center of the castle, where the gallery rises up three floors to a domed ceiling with opaque glass and iron ribs between the panes.

The gallery is always busy with servants running back and forth with meals or messages or both and courtiers waiting for a chance at any of the royal family.

This morning is no different. In fact, I would say the gallery is busier than usual.

I spot Hally leaning against the mane of the stone lion sculpture that sits at the base of the stone balustrade. He's laughing, conversing with the group of courtesans that have gathered around him.

He doesn't look at all like he's suffering from stomach pain.

I hurry around the mezzanine to the grand staircase, but Asha pulls me to a stop.

"What are you going to say to him?" she whispers.

Even though she and I were both running down the same set of stairs, there is not a hint of sweat on her face. By contrast, I feel sticky along my spine and a little damp on my forehead.

If I go down there looking like this, the entire court will be talking about how the queen was sweaty and in a rush to see the Crown Prince, which will do me no favors.

Hally and I look the same age and there have been countless rumors in court that have alleged of our affair. The only reason there is any life to them is because we are often spotted in shadows in heated conversations.

But if anyone knew what we were actually saying to one another, the rumors of an affair would be laughed out of court.

Most of the time, Hally and I are telling each other just how much we can't stand the other.

If I could murder him and get away with it, I would.

He thinks I married his father for money and to steal the crown from him. When really, I was never given a choice. King Hald made it clear that if I wanted to live, I would become his wife.

Looking back, I can't help but wonder if Hald knew more than I did about what I was capable of. He saw something in me very early on, something he could exploit. And I let him because I was desperate to feel safe. Eventually he and I came to an understanding, eventually I came to even enjoy his company.

But now he is dying and I am left once again to fend for myself.

Every morning I wake in a panic, wondering if I'm dead or about to be dead. I barely sleep anymore. How can I when Hally is slowly assembling a cohort of people who want to see me gone?

The whispers of our illicit affair have slowly, over time, morphed to something worse: they think I'm one of the *vermis,* an evil witch come to influence their court.

There is no safe space for me within the castle walls, especially now.

Asha pulls a silk handkerchief from her vest pocket and hands it to me. I dab at my forehead, then sweep back my hair, smoothing it into submission.

"If he's done something I should be worried about, he'll tell me of his own accord," I say to Asha. "And I have to know."

Her mouth is a straight line, her expression closed off. But she gives me a quick nod, backing me up.

"Do I look put together?" I ask her.

She takes the handkerchief back and it disappears into her vest pocket. "Take a breath," she instructs.

I suck in one, shoulders rocking back, then breathe it out, low and slow.

"Better," she decides and then I turn for the stairs and make my way down.

When the gathered crowd spots me, they immediately go quiet and assemble into a line, their hands clasped before them, heads bowed.

Hally pushes away from the stone lion. There is a glow about him, like he's gotten away with something, and my stomach sinks.

"Your Majesty," Hally says and gives me a shallow bow.

The assembled line at least has the decency to bow in the way that is expected when standing before a queen.

They all murmur good morning to me but avoid making eye contact.

"Good morning to you all," I say, keeping my voice light and airy. Even before the rumors that I am a witch, the court liked to call me a cold-hearted bitch behind my back because I often avoid court gatherings, and when I do attend, I keep to myself.

I can't stomach the gossip and the small talk.

"And how are you this morning, Hally?"

He gives me a tight smile, teeth locked together. He hates it when I call him Hally, his father's nickname for him.

"I'm well, Your Majesty. And you? I suspect you're feeling cheerful and lively, what with your visiting companions?"

The assembled group perks up.

Now it's my turn to smile with gnashed teeth.

"Companions?" I say because I don't want to give away that they mean anything at all to me.

"The two men who visited your private room earlier this morning?"

The whispers between the courtesans is practically sparking with fire.

"Handsome men, both of them. I had a chance to greet them at the gate. We couldn't let our dear queen's friends slip away without supper. Lucky I caught them in time."

Ice cold. That's what I am. Ice *fucking* cold.

"If you're referring to the two men who were escorted in by the Captain of the Guard, you'll be disappointed to learn that they were looking for someone else and were sent away to continue their quest for their missing friend."

Hally's nostrils flare and he steps forward, shrinking the distance between us. He's far too close, even for a prince. Everyone knows social decorum says to give the queen a wide berth.

"Whatever the case may be," he goes on, "they gladly accepted the supper invitation."

Goddamn them.

"So if their friend is here in our court," Hally adds, "we'll find out soon enough."

With that, he swivels around and walks away, the heels of his leather boots clacking loudly on the marble floor.

CHAPTER FIFTEEN
ROC

W<small>E ARE ESCORTED UP A BACK STAIRCASE BY A SERVANT, THEN</small> deposited into two connecting rooms. We're told supper is at six-sharp and that we're to see the court tailor at two for more appropriate attire.

I'm always in the mood to be pampered.

When the servant is gone and I'm alone, I walk the perimeter of the room, taking in the details.

It's appointed well with a stone hearth and a large mantle. An oil painting framed in a gilded frame hangs above, depicting a medieval battle between the witches and one of Everland's many kings.

Next to the hearth, is a desk, then two red velvet wing-back chairs that sit beside a wall of windows that overlook the castle's inner courtyard.

The bed is square against the wall I now share with the Captain and directly across from it is a door leading to a washroom.

Tucked behind the door, I find a bar cart stocked with brandy and rum.

I make my way there and pour myself a shot.

Glass in hand, I go to the wingback, drop into it, and light a cigarette.

Is there anything more comforting than velvet and burning tobacco and warm brandy?

I think not.

The door connecting my room with the Captain's rattles from the other side but the lock holds fast.

"Beast!" the Captain yells. "Open the door."

I take a swill from my glass.

The door handle turns back and forth.

"Roc!"

I close my eyes and rest my head against one of the chair's curved sides. The sun is pouring in through the windows now, warming the velvet.

The Captain lets out a disgruntled sigh, and then his footsteps stalk from the door, out into the hallway, and then he's bursting into my room.

"Why didn't you unlock the door?"

I open my eyes.

He steps back.

My mother said I came out of the womb with eyes as bright as jade.

My father would tell me, "Every time you looked at her, she would mark herself with an X to ward off evil."

He was boasting, of course. But that wasn't how ten-year-old me took it.

Ten-year-old me believed that the reason his mother threw herself off a cliff was because she couldn't stand to exist beneath the gaze of her eldest son.

I know my attention is both the bait and a weapon.

I try to use it responsibly but sometimes I forget.

The Captain licks his lips. He gets control of himself and

turns to his frustration because it's always easier to be angry than it is to be flustered.

"Beast," he says like it's a curse word.

"Why didn't I open the door?" I repeat back to him. "Because I didn't feel like it."

He grumbles and his dark brow forms a V over his eyes.

The Captain is used to bossing people around and I think the fact that I would rather eat rocks than be commanded makes him bratty.

And a bratty Captain has me feeling feelings I'd rather not feel. Like the desire to throw him onto the bed and blow that frustration right off his face.

Innuendo fucking intended.

But I've already taken his hand. How much more can I devour?

And for that matter, how much of Wendy can I take?

For the first time in my entire fucking life, I am seeded with doubt.

I don't like it.

I take a hit from the cigarette and let the smoke create a veil over my eyes.

The Captain goes on, muttering about my lackadaisical nature and how it will be my undoing. He gestures with his hand and hook as he talks, pointing the sharp tine at me.

"Are you even listening to me?" he says a few minutes later.

"I'm sorry, what?"

With a sigh, he goes to the bar and pours himself a drink and slings it back in one gulp.

I watch as his Adam's apple bobs in his throat and fire ignites in my chest.

He sets the glass down and shuts the door with the curve of his hook. When he returns to me, he lowers his voice. "Whatever we're doing here, it seems like a bad idea. Something isn't right."

He's correct about that.

Something has changed about our Darling, Wendy. She's different but I can't quite put my finger on how yet.

"What is your plan?" the Captain asks.

"Plan? You think too highly of me. There is no plan."

He gives me a look like I've just greatly disturbed him. "You must be joking."

"Must I?"

He huffs out.

I take another hit, exhale.

"Why don't you seem worried?" he asks.

"Worrying is for nuns and rabbits."

"What...*what the bloody hell*!" He lifts his arms and then lets them drop dramatically to his sides. "You are impossible."

"I think you mean impeccable."

"No I don't!"

"Perhaps impenetrable? No that's not right either. I am definitely *penetrable*." I give him a grin. He crosses his arms over his chest, his hook sticking out, and he inhales long and deep.

He makes it far too easy.

I take another draw from the cigarette and hold the smoke in my lungs.

"Something is wrong," he says again, lower, more incessantly.

I exhale a purposeful breath and the smoke clouds in a beam of sunlight. "I know," I tell him and his shoulders drop with relief.

Grounding out the cigarette in a nearby ashtray, I get up

and meet him on the rug. "Wendy was afraid and it wasn't of us."

The Captain frowns. "How do you know?"

"I could hear it in her heartbeat first, and in the tremor in her voice second."

His frown deepens. "You think she's in danger?"

"Very much so. And I would bet it has something to do with the Crown Prince."

The Captain nods and paces away, his arms now clasped behind his back. "The prince isn't her son?"

"No, but it does beg many questions. How long has Wendy been queen? Does he hold a grudge against his stepmother? And most importantly, where the fuck is the king?"

"Wendy's husband, you mean."

"Yes, that idiot."

He glances at me and speaks what we've both been thinking. "Do you suppose she had a choice in this marriage?"

"When does a woman ever have a choice when it comes to kings?"

The Captain grits his teeth.

I share his same anger, but I just hide mine better. No sense showing my cards. *Yet.*

The anger will show it's face when it needs to, when the moment counts.

"What are we going to do? This is far more complicated than I thought."

I walk to the windows that overlook the courtyard below. Some castles only use their courtyards for function and practicality. Livestock and water reserves and crop storage. Everland's is for show. Well manicured gardens and a giant stone fountain in the center. From up here, it's easier to see the trimmed boxwood hedges were planted to form an intricate design of swirls and arches.

There are people milling about, women in ornate dresses carrying lace parasols and men in linen coats smoking as they walk.

All of it is normal enough, but there is an underlying thread of *something* here.

"We'll attend this supper tonight," I tell him. "And then we'll know more."

"And if we are walking into a trap?"

I turn around and smile at him. "Oh Captain. You should know by now, crocodiles are very hard to catch."

CHAPTER SIXTEEN
WENDY

THE KING'S BEDROOM SMELLS OF CAMPHOR AND TALLOW CANDLES.

The drapes are pulled closed making the room feel oppressively heavy and dark.

There are two nurses at his side. They bow to me and exit through the only other door, one hidden behind a large tapestry that leads straight to the healer's quarters.

Since he slipped into a coma two months ago, King Hald has been under constant watch.

I go to his bed and sit on the wooden stool left by one of the nurses. On the bedside table, a candle, in its bronze holder, flickers with my movement, the flame going sideways.

The dancing light casts eerie shadows over the dying Everland king.

His head is nestled in a dip in his feather pillow, the thick brocade blanket pulled up to his neck. His mouth is hanging open and every breath he takes makes his chest sink in, and then rattles his lungs on the exit.

"When will you wake up?" I whisper. "I am like a fly caught in a web and I can't help but feel you helped spin it."

I laugh, but it's full of despair. "Perhaps that is too harsh. I knew what I was signing up for. I just never could have foreseen *this*."

I reach over, gripping his thin arm through the blanket. "Please, Hald. I need you more than ever. I don't know what to do."

The flame flickers again.

Out of the corner of my eye, I see the tapestry lift as the door opens. Footsteps sound on the stone floor.

Hally comes into the bloom of light cast by the candle.

He looks so much like his father — mildly handsome with thick blond hair, a sharp jaw, a thin Everland nose and dark, deep brown eyes.

When I married his father, we were the same age, Hally and I. His father was twice our age and chronically ill with disease.

But then Hald recovered, and then he stopped aging.

That's when the whispers began. That the king had struck a deal with the fae. Or maybe he drank from a fairy fountain. Or the worst, that he married a witch, *meaning me*.

Hald quickly squashed the rumors by declaring himself marked by the gods. And who would ever be bold enough to call a king a liar?

Once the gossiping quieted, I thought we were safe, even though Hally made it quite clear he still thought me either a con-woman or a witch.

I didn't think his opinion mattered because he'd be long dead before his father.

I should have known better. Hally is too resourceful, too ambitious.

If his father wasn't going to age, then neither was he.

I haven't a clue how he managed it though.

I have my suspicions. Just no concrete proof.

"Your Majesty," he says and gives me a shallow bow.

"Your Highness," I say in return.

Hally goes to the foot of the bed and leans against the thick post, crossing his legs at the ankles. "I didn't mean to eavesdrop," he says.

"I'm sure."

"I overheard you pleading with my father to wake, that you didn't know what to do. But dear stepmother. I am here for you. I know it must be difficult, running this country as a woman. It is a job that was never meant for the more fragile sex."

I roll my eyes.

"Step down and allow me to fill the role of co-regent and you can return to your leisure time."

The nerve of this asshole.

I let go of Hald and stand up, shoulders and back straight. "If the role was never meant for a woman, then why did your father revise the royal code? Why did he make me heir to the throne in the event of his..." I swallow. "His incapacitation or departure?"

This, *this* is the web I am trapped in.

Once Hally stopped aging, Hald accused him of courting the *vermes* and changed the line of succession, giving the throne to me.

I thought he would be around forever and saying yes wouldn't matter. I thought I could help him, no matter what danger or treachery he faced.

I was wrong.

Now, not only is Hald in a coma, but everyone in court is looking at me like I somehow caused it because I am the one who stands to gain the most.

But I didn't do this.

I never wanted to rule. I saw the stress the highest seat in the land caused my husband.

You would be a fool to want that position.

I could do as Hally asks — I could denounce my position and hand over the reins to him. But I made Hald a promise.

That, and I'm not entirely sure having Hally in charge is for the good of the land.

Why must I have a conscience?

Everland has never loved me. So why the hell do I feel a responsibility to it?

I look over at Hald as he struggles for another breath.

Perhaps, in some way, my responsibility is to him.

He is a decent man. Despite the way I came to be his wife, he still always treated me with respect and decency.

It's more than I can say for James or Roc.

In fact, Hald and I never even consummated our marriage because Hald knew I didn't feel that way about him and I was more than happy to look the other way when he took on one or more mistresses.

"The answer is simple," Hally finally says.

"And what's that?"

"My father wasn't in his right mind."

I snort.

"Either that, or you twisted his mind."

"I would never, so you have no proof."

"It's only a matter of time, *Wendy*." He bites out my name like it's a curse and I sense the approaching spider.

I turn for the door. "I'll leave you to your private time with your father. Good day, Your Highness."

"I look forward to getting to know our special guests tonight. I'm sure they'll have much to say about their old friend Wendy Darling."

CHAPTER SEVENTEEN
WENDY

Asha goes to the royal practice yard every day after the mid-day meal and so it's easy to find her when I need her. She's in the center of the ring using one of the practice dummies for sword work. Her speed is unmatched within the royal army and she's cut several new notches into the wood in the handful of minutes I watch her from the fence.

"Care for a partner?" I ask her.

She sheaths her sword and comes over. "It's never good to wield a blade when you're distracted."

I unhook the iron latch on the gate and enter the ring.

The royal practice yard is behind the castle but within the curtain wall. It's tucked between a tall hedge row and the giant Wonderland oak known as the Scarlet Giant. Only the higher-ranking soldiers from the army or those with direct permission from the royal family are allowed to utilize the more private yard.

"Practice swords then?" I ask Asha and she finally gives me a nod.

I select one from the storage cabinet and spin it around

the way Asha taught me, warming up my muscles and my muscle memory.

For mid-day, it's rather dark and gloomy and the air is crisp. There is no one else around and we're far enough away from the castle that it would be hard to spot us from a window.

I'm grateful for the reprieve.

I've changed into my fighting trousers and the tight-fitting tunic. It feels good to be out of that damnable dress. I've never loved the traditional attire for a queen. I would much rather dress like a man, but Everland customs frown on it.

"Are you ready, Your Majesty?" Asha asks, stretching out her neck, then rolling her shoulders.

"I'm ready."

There was a time when I believed myself to be weak. When I sat in that prison cell in the Tower, wishing for someone to save me, I thought that was the only way I would escape.

Training with Asha has given me more confidence. When I admitted my fears of my own inadequacies to her, she told me, "If you know how to properly knee a man in the balls, you will never be without a weapon." And I've held on to that all these years later.

I take my fighting stance and Asha circles me.

The fighting begins.

It's always been impossible for me to keep up with her. Her movements are fluid but calculated. They are the practiced movements of a woman who grew up with a sword in hand.

I am envious of Asha most days even though I suspect that what brought her here was pain and despair.

She never speaks of her family or her life in the Winterland Mountains and who am I to press? There are secrets about my past that even she doesn't know.

I suspect that's why we trust each other so much—we are not ones to pry for secrets we have not earned.

The flat of Asha's practice blade catches me across the shoulder and I hiss out in pain, trying not to let it distract me.

Asha pulls back because I'm the queen and she'll never give me her full might even if I beg for it.

Using the footwork she pounded into me for weeks and months, I get in a jab to her ribs, then aim with a slicing motion on the back of her thigh. She catches me though, blocking the blow and our wooden swords let out a loud crack.

"You are still distracted," she tells me, not the least bit winded.

"I am not," I argue and swing the blade around over my head, then cut down in a diagonal. She blocks. We separate and dance back, circling one another.

I'm determined to prove to her that I'm not distracted, and feint left, then pull back to the right with the edge of my blade.

But Asha has her own plans and steps into my guard.

The clash of movements results in my sword whacking her across the knuckles and the hilt of her sword hitting me just below the eye.

The blow sends a shockwave down my neck and I stumble back as Asha cradles her hand to her chest.

"Are you okay?" I ask her, my cheek still smarting.

"Of course I am."

I let my sword drop to the dirt. "Let me see."

"Wendy," she says in an admonishing tone that only Asha can get away with.

"Just let me see it."

With a sigh, she holds her arm out before her.

There is a sizable bruise blooming across her knuckles with the middle swollen twice it's size like it may be cracked.

"I'm so sorry."

"Don't be foolish," she says. "We were fighting. It isn't as if you escaped unharmed."

Instinctively, I bring my own hand to my eye and then wince when my fingertips hit tender flesh.

"I'll be fine."

"It's a black eye. People will talk."

I don't bother reminding her that it will heal within the hour. It's one more of those secrets we don't talk about outright for fear of the truth of it.

I take her hand in my left, then cover her knuckles with my right.

I don't even have to think about it anymore — my power comes easily.

The air takes on the smell of vetiver and wet moss and fresh cut flowers.

Heat radiates out from both of my palms and Asha lets out a contented sigh.

When I let her go, the bruise is gone, the knuckle no longer swollen.

"Thank you," she says and rubs at the spot.

It's this secret, mysterious power that got me onto the throne. But it wasn't until I was hung for treason and then refused to die that even I became aware of it.

Ultimately, this power saved my life not once, but twice. The first time from the end of a noose. The second time when King Hald made me a deal—heal him, become his wife, dedicate my power to him and only him, and he would make me queen.

I had never felt safe. Not even as a child. I had always known Peter Pan would come for me. His specter haunted me until one night, he was finally there, tearing me away from my home.

Hald had given me something I had never known: safety and security.

And so I agreed, lending him my power for decades and then some.

Until one day my power no longer worked on him.

And like a dam breaking, his illness and his age washed through.

Within days, he was bedridden, within weeks, he was comatose.

"I don't understand why it works on you but not him," I say.

Asha picks up her practice blade. "You know I come from a practical village. They embraced action, not magic. So take of this what you will: if I had to guess, something is blocking you."

Yes but what? Am I self-sabotaging?

Deep down, I am afraid that maybe the rumors are true. Maybe I am a dark witch, maybe I possess something rotten at the core.

Maybe I deserve everything that's coming my way.

And if my future promises only death and destruction, I have to do everything in my power to drive James and Roc away so they aren't swept up in the mess that has become my life.

CHAPTER EIGHTEEN
HOOK

A̲FTER DOZING THE AFTERNOON, I'M ROUSED FROM BED BY A mustached servant knocking on my door. He's dressed in court livery and informs me I'm to report to the court tailor. When I come out into the hallway, Roc is nowhere to be found and when I ask the servant when he will join us, he says the Crocodile's appointment isn't until much later.

I try not to let this disappoint me, but somehow it does.

The servant takes me down a series of hallways, then down the main staircase where it spills out to the mezzanine. From there, we cross into the opposite wing of the castle and finally he deposits me at the arched door of the tailor.

With a bow, and a farewell, the servant is gone.

The door is slightly ajar so I give it a push and peer inside. "Hello?"

There are several wooden dress forms in the receiving room, all holding up dresses in silk and chiffon.

"Hello?" I call again and a man appears in a second doorway at the back of the room. He's wearing a gold brocade vest over a white shirt with lace trimmed around the sleeve cuffs. There is a pinched appearance to his face, as if his god made him, then pressed his cheeks together.

"I heard you the first time!" he says.

"Apologies." I give him a bow. "I wasn't sure if anyone was here."

The man comes over, his gaze immediately assessing my body.

"Hmm." His eyes narrow and he brings one hand to his chin as if in deep thought. His fingernails are cut short, his fingertips callused, likely from hours and hours of sewing by hand.

"Narrow shoulders. Broad chest." He clucks his tongue. "You're not well-proportioned."

"And who decides?"

He tilts his head, gazing up at me. "Well then." A tape measure appears in his hand and he unravels it with a snap. "Arms up."

I do as he instructs and he measures my chest.

"I'm not a magician, you'll know. I can't pull a suit out of thin air, so I have to source something from the royal closet. Proportions mean everything in a fitting, do they not?"

"Well, I'm not sure—"

"They do!" He measures my waist next, then my hips. "What's your inseam?"

"Thirty-two."

"Hmm," he says again and then steps back. "I'd consider you a deep winter."

"A *what*?"

He murmurs to himself and then disappears through the door where he first appeared.

I follow him, stopping just over the threshold.

It's hard to fathom the size of this inner closet from the

receiving room. It's like opening a clam shell and finding the vastness of the ocean inside.

The closet is twice the size of my ballroom back in Neverland. There are rows and rows of clothing racks, then dressers, then shelves, then more racks. Suits and dresses and coats and tunics as far as the eye can see.

The man flips through several hangers.

"Deep winter," he says, pulling out a navy blue suit and then deciding against it. "That's your color palette. You stick to deep winter colors and you'll always look stunning."

"What does that entail?"

"Well, first, stop with the gold." He waves his hand in my general direction.

I glance down. My jacket has gold buttons and gold trim around the cuffs. My belt buckle is also gold.

"I like gold."

"You can like it. Just don't wear it." He pulls out another outfit. "Silver will suit you better. Trust me." He shows me his selection. It's a dark charcoal frock tailcoat with military-inspired silver embroidery along the lapel and silver epaulets. He pairs it with charcoal trousers and leather boots that would rest just below my knees.

"Changing room through there." He nods at another door tucked between two clothing racks. "Try it on and then come out."

Once inside, I shut the door behind me and then hang the clothes on several hooks screwed into the wall.

There is a full-length mirror in the corner, set on its own gilded stand. My reflection stares back at me.

Is gold really not my color?

I turn, assessing for myself. I don't see it.

But when I slip out of my normal clothes and into the

military frock coat, it's immediately apparent. The tailor is right.

The silver looks much better and the shade of charcoal, with just a hint of dark blue in it, contrasts nicely with my complexion.

The first stupid thought to pop into my head is, *That damnable beast will surely admire the cut of this suit against my body.*

And then I snatch the thought back and shove it down as far as it will go.

We are mortal enemies. Even if he did give me one of the best blow jobs I've ever had. Maybe more so. It still feels like a trick. Like a drug dealer who has given me a taste of a drug he and I both know I can never taste again.

Roc did warn me, didn't he?

You'll never be the same after.

I slip on the boots, then step out. "I'm ready," I call and the tailor pops his head out from between two racks of suits.

"Ahhh, yes! Much better." He uses a sturdy brush to pull off any lint or stray threads, then straightens the silver tassels that hang from the epaulets.

"Brilliant," he decides.

"Thank you," I say.

"Now off to the coiffurist with you."

"*Now?*"

"Yes. Is there a better time?" He pushes me into the receiving room, then back out into the hallway, proving that there isn't, and also that he never expected an answer anyway. My original escort, the servant with the mustache, is already waiting for me.

He leads me down another hall, then another, and I'm

quickly whisked into a room lined on one side with tall windows that let in the bright light of late afternoon.

I'm deposited in a plush leather chair and a man and woman, speaking in a language I don't understand, descend on me. My hair is brushed, then combed, then mussed with thick paste that smells of mint and lemongrass. The man shaves me clean, while the woman tames any flyaways with the soft touch of her fingers.

When they're finished, they chatter with one another over me, nodding and smiling.

"Handsome," the man says.

"Hot," the woman says.

"Thank you," I say again because I suppose if I'm to have supper with Wendy Darling, *the queen*, I really should look my best.

Once I leave the coiffurist, the mustached servant leads me back to the mezzanine where people are already starting to arrive for supper.

At the grand staircase, the servant bows, gestures for me to go down, then leaves me.

There is a crowd in the grand foyer and I attract their attention as soon as I descend the stairs.

I don't see Wendy and I don't see Roc. The servant may very well be escorting him to the tailor now. But without any familiar faces, I'm left to fend for myself.

But I'm not left alone for long.

The Crown Prince appears at my side when I hit the marble floor. There is a woman tucked behind him like an afterthought.

"Captain James Hook," the prince says.

"Your Highness." I give him the required bow.

"You clean up nicely." He regards me from boot to jaw. "Our court tailor and coiffurist really are unmatched. I suppose there's nothing like it on your wild island of Neverland."

He's right, of course, but I detect the dismissive in the words he's chosen.

"Thank you kindly for the hospitality. I did not pack for supper with Everland royalty."

"Of course. It's our pleasure."

The woman behind him is hidden partially in the shadow of the lion stone statue, and the rise of the prince's shoulder.

Is he married? Courting? Fucking around?

When he catches me noticing his companion, he seems to remember suddenly that he has one. "Oh right. Allow me to introduce you to my betrothed. Lady Mareth Shade."

He holds out his hand for her and her pale fingers slip into his palm. He pulls her around and into the light.

And I am immediately confused by the pretty face of the girl.

She seems so familiar.

Her nose is thin and pointed, her eyes big and bright. There is a mole just above the left corner of her mouth. A dark star in an otherwise pale expanse.

"Have we met?" I ask her.

She looks down, hiding her eyes. "I don't believe so, sir."

I wrack my brain, trying to place her.

"Did you spend any time on Neverland? Perhaps on the northern port?"

The prince laughs. "My beautiful bride-to-be would never visit such an untamed land."

The girl laughs with him and then loops her arm through his, positioning herself half behind him again.

She is demure, innocent and beautiful. All the things that are expected of a woman about to marry a prince.

"Apologies." I give the girl and the prince a bow. "I must be mistaken."

The prince covers the girl's hand with his. "Now if you'll excuse us. We'll look forward to seeing you at the supper table, Captain Hook. I can't wait to hear more of your history with my stepmother."

The way he says it—stepmother—leads me to believe what he'd like to say is step-monster. Clearly no love is lost between them.

And I know just how to play this. "I assure you, Your Highness, there isn't much history to speak of. We knew each other for a brief moment a long time ago. I just happened to be passing through and thought to ask after her."

He smiles, gives the girl a pat. "Just as well."

With a nod, they turn from me and join another crowd nearer the dining hall.

But I can't help but watch the girl as they greet more of the court.

I'm quite sure I'm not mistaken, but my memory is drawing a blank at placing her.

Perhaps Roc will know her. At his indeterminable age, it seems like he knows everyone and if *I* know *him*, he'll enjoy the game of trying to figure it out.

CHAPTER NINETEEN
WENDY

When my handmaid had asked me what dress I preferred for tonight's supper, I told her anything would do so long as it had pockets.

And now, as I walk down the long galley that leads to the supper hall, I rub at the warm selenite stone hidden in my left pocket. It was a gift given to me by a woman I shared a cell with in the Everland Tower Prison.

"For your worries," she'd said and opened her palm to reveal the smooth crystal with it's well-worn divot, perfect for the pad of any thumb.

I don't know if there's any truth to rocks and crystals having healing powers or metaphysical properties, but it's always helped distract me from anxiety and so it's a tool I've clung to ever since I cowered in that cold, dank prison cell.

Somedays, the terror of returning to that place threatens to swallow me whole. Somedays it's so bad, I have to remain in my room sipping borsha tea just to calm my nerves.

Somedays I truly believe I am forever destined to be someone's prisoner, in a cell or in a kingdom.

I enter the supper hall and the room goes silent and still.

This is normal. To be expected. But it still makes my skin crawl.

I don't like to be noticed.

I grip the selenite so tightly, I'm worried it may crack.

"Her Majesty, Queen Wendellyn," the court herald calls out.

Wendellyn is the name Hald bestowed on me when he decided I would be his bride and not a former prisoner with supposed allegiances to Peter Pan.

Even though Pan abandoned me on Everland, his motives mattered not. I had ties to him. So I was guilty by association.

Hald told me I needed to erase every semblance of my past, including my name.

And so Wendellyn was born.

Hald provided me with fake documentation that said I was a distant cousin of Queen Annabella from Southern Winterland, which made me fit to marry a king.

That story persisted until Hally decided to go digging. He eventually uncovered my origin story and my birth name. Why he hasn't shared it with the entire court is beyond me. I can't help but feel like he's reserving it as a weapon to use against me, like a bomb he plans to set off when the mood strikes.

With my arrival officially announced, I make my way down the red carpet that runs from the entrance across the entire supper hall to the royal table at the head of the room where behind it, a giant oil painting of myself and Hald hangs from wire and an iron spike. We sat for hours for that painting. It did not escape my notice that the artist made Hald look younger than he actually was, a little trimmer around the waist, while my nose was done in sharper strokes, my eyes narrowed with cruelty.

Hald said it made me look regal. He did have a knack for making me feel like my worries were silly.

Everyone in attendance, some three hundred people of the Everland nobility and aristocracy, are lined up on either side of the red carpet, bowing their heads, dipping into a curtsey, as I pass.

When I reach the table, I give the prince and his betrothed a nod of deference and then take my seat, the queen's chair, behind the long royal supper table.

There is a sudden pang of sadness, seeing Hald's chair beside me, empty.

Seated now, the music starts up again and the court returns to their pre-supper chatter.

A servant pours me a glass of wine. My handmaid tastes it. We wait the required minute before deeming it safe.

When she remains upright, unaffected, I take the drink and sip.

"You look resplendent tonight, Your Majesty," Hally says, lifting his chalice.

"As do you, Your Highness. That color of blue matches your eyes quite well."

He smiles. "My betrothed picked it out for me."

"You did well then, Lady Mareth," I tell her.

She smiles, dipping her chin. Her voice is barely audible above the din. "Many thanks, Your Majesty."

When Hally announced his engagement to Mareth, I truly thought he was joking. Mareth is the daughter of some lesser noble I can never remember the name of. She is barely pretty, not that that should matter. But with Hally I imagined there would be no greater requirement. Though perhaps he wishes to be the prettier of the match. He does like attention. I suppose it makes sense that he doesn't want his bride to steal his spotlight.

"Have you seen our honored guests yet?" Hally scans the supper hall and my heart beats a little harder.

"You invited them, Your Highness. I would have expected you'd keep track of them."

When my handmaid asked after my dress preference, I should have added *no whalebone corset*. Because right now I'm finding it difficult to breathe against the ribbing. It's making me peevish.

But if Hally is put off by my attitude, he gives no indication of it.

"I'm sure they'll turn up soon enough," he says. "Oh look, speak of the devil."

I follow Hally's gaze to the supper hall's entrance and my shoulders drop with relief.

The herald calls out, "Captain James Hook."

James gives the herald a nod, then clasps his arms behind his back, entering the supper hall with all the grace of an Englishman who feels right at home.

I am relieved he is the first to arrive.

I think it's possible James and I are cut from the same type of fabric. Both fine fabric with delicate stitching and very specific uses. We are the type of fabric meant to drape, not form.

I understand James.

I have never understood Roc.

He is like a summer storm blowing in out of nowhere, unpredictable in nature, at times violent and so darkly beautiful, it makes your eyes burn.

James I can handle. There is no such thing as handling

Roc. You can only hold on tightly and hope he doesn't consume you whole.

James makes the required greetings and then he's spotted me at the head of the hall and the way he looks at me, it's like he's spotted land for the first time in ages.

My heart kicks up again.

Butterflies fill my stomach.

He makes his way to me with determination.

"Your Majesty." He bows. I notice his arms are still clasped behind him, hiding his hook. Does he worry about frightening me?

When we were together, he had both hands and by the gods, did he know how to use them.

James's touch was always gentle, warm and passionate.

By contrast, Roc's touch was bruising and possessive.

If I were a respectable girl, I would say I preferred James's touch.

But I am not.

If pressed to choose, I couldn't.

Which is exactly why I found myself torn between them all those years ago. I wanted them both for different reasons, in different ways.

I was always the rose bush, both soft and sharp.

All these years later, and I think I have not changed.

I want to be terrified by Roc. I want to be adored by James.

I want it all, all of it and more.

And knowing I can never have it makes my heart break all over again.

They should have left.

No, *they never should have come.*

James and I stare at one another. He's clearly been to the royal closet. He's dressed in a fine tailcoat with silver handiwork done by none other than Bittershore the Tailor.

Bitter is half fae, though the court will not admit to it. The court frowns on anything magical, unless the magic makes us look good.

Truly, there is no one better with a needle than he. And James is benefiting from Bitter's eye and his craft.

The tailcoat fits James as if it were sewn especially for him and the military style gives him command and presence.

I imagine after Bitter, he was sent to the Whitdrey twins, the royal coiffurist, because he's been clean-shaven, his hair styled and tamed.

He looks dashing and it doesn't escape me that most of the court is assessing him with hungry eyes, both men and women.

And if all eyes of the court weren't on us, I would pull him aside and I would sink into his warmth and pry his secrets from his lips.

Why is he here now? Why is he with Roc, his mortal enemy?

And then I would warn him.

You must escape this maddening place, I'd tell him. *Before it kills you.*

"Your Majesty," James says, "your beauty rivals the sun."

Hally snorts beside me and James's jaw clenches at the sound.

"You flatter me," I respond because it's what's expected.

"James," Hally says. "As our honored guest, we've given you a seat at our table. You'll join us in a position of honor, to the right of the king's chair."

James eyes the empty chair beside me, then the two

further down. The last must be meant for Roc. If he ever decides to show up. Fashionably late, as always. If I didn't know better, I'd guess he was in some coat closet fucking a servant.

And the thought makes my stomach turn sour.

It makes me want to smash things.

He better not be fucking anyone under my roof.

Oh calm down! He doesn't belong to you. He never did.

"I would, of course, be honored," James says and gives another shallow bow to the prince before taking his seat on the other side of Hald's.

But it's impossible to converse with him, what with a large chair between us.

My nerves prickle as I consider how I might remedy that.

Of course, all of this is a game and I know Hally has been playing it since James and Roc stepped foot on Everland soil and started asking for Wendy Darling.

So why not play the game with him?

I wave over one of the pages. He bows and waits for my command.

"Could you please remove the king's chair so that I may properly converse with our honored guests?"

Though I am facing away from Hally, I can feel his ire like a sharp winter's frost.

I know this is a dangerous move.

But I want to remind him that I don't always play by the rules.

The page sputters for a second then nods and says, "Of course, Your Majesty." Then he wrestles the chair away from the table, pulling it back to the wall.

"Come, James," I say. "Join me."

James gets up. The page moves his chair to my side and

then one of the servants shuffles down the table settings, both for James and for Roc.

"There," I say and smile over at Hally. "That's better."

The vein running down the center of Hally's forehead bulges against his skin. Lady Mareth sets her pale, delicate hand on his thigh and gives him a reassuring squeeze. Some of his tension fades.

I will pay for this later. But right now, it's worth it.

James's glass is filled. I waggle my finger at my handmaid, and she tests his drink.

James gives me a look, but I pretend not to notice.

"Are you being treated well?" I ask him.

He licks his lips. I remember kissing them. I remember the tender way his mouth met mine, the hungry way his tongue took a taste of me.

For the first time in a very long time, there is a flash of heat between my legs and it catches me so off guard, I blush.

"Your court's generosity knows no bounds," James says.

I scan the supper hall. People are slowly making their way to their tables.

"Where is Roc?"

James groans. "I wish I could tell you."

I sip from my chalice. So they are not so close that they are intimately aware of the comings and goings of the other.

I will admit, seeing them together, there was a pang of envy. I think I am jealous of anyone who gets to exist in their orbit.

Seeing them on their knees, shoulders touching, I wanted to be angry at James for being where I wish I could be, and at Roc for having what I'd always wanted in James. But of course, that's ridiculous.

It's not like they're together *together*.

I cut a glance at James. It occurs to me, suddenly, that I may have misread their closeness as perfunctory.

What if there is more between them?

What if I am the odd one out?

And just when I think that perhaps I'm making it up in my mind, more paranoia than fact, Roc walks into the room and James sits up straighter, his breathing shifting, more shallow, *excited*.

He swallows, his Adam's apple sinking in his perfect, beautiful throat.

And my stomach drops.

No. *No*.

The jealousy springs up, threatening to drown me.

"The...ahem, *Crocodile*," the herald calls.

The hush that goes over the crowd can only be described as *buzzing*.

It's like the king himself has walked into the supper hall.

While Roc may not be royalty, he does have a reputation.

If you are not charmed by his charm, or enraptured by his beauty, you are terrified of his power.

It's impossible not to be alert when the Crocodile walks into the room.

We are all caught by him now and he knows it. While it's impossible to handle Roc, Roc knows exactly how to handle *us*.

He smiles at the court with all his perfect white teeth, sharp incisors flashing.

My breath stutters down my throat.

He, too, has been to visit Bitter. But while Bitter dressed James in an elegant military suit, he knew that anything embellished would only detract from Roc's beauty.

He's wearing an unadorned black suit that skims his body in all the right ways.

Beside me, James sighs and I glance back at him.

"This is always what I hated most about him," he admits, his voice low and hoarse.

"What?" I coax.

"How damn good he looks in a suit."

My jaw drops a little, nose burning.

If I needed any further proof, here it is.

By some twist of fate or magic, the once mortal enemies are now indulging in one another and I am barred from them, a queen in name, but a beggar still, looking for scraps of the only two men who ever made me feel something.

Why did I ever leave them?

Some nights while I lay in that cold, wet dungeon, I would silently sob in the dark, asking myself why I had chosen to run away.

Looking back, I know why I thought it was the right decision. Roc and Pan had already terrorized Hook, taking his hand simply for daring to touch me. And the whole reason I was with Hook was because he kidnapped me from Pan, looking to settle a score.

I wanted no part of their violence or their war. I wanted to love. I wanted to feel safe.

I think a little part of me thought that one of them would chase me, proving their devotion.

What a stupid, vapid girl I had been.

Roc saunters through the crowd, flirting with the entire court as he makes his way to the royal table.

Every step he takes, every foot of distance he closes

between us, my heart beats a little harder until it's hot and hammering in my ears.

I still feel like that stupid, vapid girl. One look from Roc and I've lost all sense.

When he finally reaches me, he stops and bows. "Your Majesty." When he straightens again, his smile is crooked and dissolute. A smile of a rogue.

"Good of you to finally join us," I say.

James chokes on a laugh beside me.

Roc never falters. "If you'll forgive me, I was caught by the beauty of your great castle." He nods at Hally. "Your Highness, I must say, your family has great taste in art and architecture. Was it Vison who designed the castle?"

Hally sputters, searching for an answer. "I believe it was, yes."

"I thought so." Roc's gaze turns to the high, arched ceiling, to the curved beams and the cherubic faces hand carved into the eaves. "It has his delightful sense of humor."

It wasn't Vison though. It was Morsoni Maracopa III. It's literally carved into the cornerstone.

When Roc's attention comes back to me, he winks.

So he knows Hally knows nothing about his own house. Leave it to Roc to play a game that only he knows he's playing.

The fact that he's pulled me into it though...

I flush again and my belly dips.

"If you'll join us at our table," Hally says, nodding at the empty seat at the other end. "Our first course is due out soon."

"Wonderful." Roc shows off his teeth again. "I'm famished."

Hook adjusts next to me, but I can't tell if it's boredom or discomfort.

Roc takes his chair on Hook's right side and once he's seated, he leans into Hook and whispers into his ear and Hook scowls at him, cursing beneath his breath.

The rest of the court settles into their seats. The band's music fills the great hall, the lyrical notes echoing above us in the beams.

We are served our first course — an aromatic creamy onion soup poured over crispy potatoes.

I have no appetite but I try to eat some of everything so as not to fuel more gossip.

Somehow I make it through all five courses. The constant stream of wine helps and by the time our dessert plate is carried away, I'm warm and buzzy and bold.

The band's tune picks up in tempo and the court fills up the dance floor.

I push back my chair. My handmaid helps me disentangle myself, straightening out the skirt of my dress.

I make my way over to Roc. "Join me in a dance."

It's not a question.

Roc and James share a look and then Roc is rising to his feet, towering over me in that dominant way he has. I always felt small next to him and that hasn't changed.

"I would be honored, Your Majesty." He takes my hand in his.

CHAPTER TWENTY
WENDY

ALL EYES ARE ON US AS ROC LEADS ME TO THE DANCE FLOOR. I HAD expected we'd melt into the crowd of assembled dancers already in the middle of an Everland reel, but as soon as I step onto the floor, the band switches tunes, the violinist taking center stage.

The first introductory notes are the notes of a lively waltz.

I must make a face because Roc says, "What's wrong, Your Majesty?"

The gleam in his eye says he already knows.

"You may remember I wasn't very good at the waltz and I'm afraid I'm no better now."

He hooks his arm around my waist, drawing me into his warmth, the solid, sturdy fold of him. He smells like an autumn night, like heady darkness and spicy warmth.

My belly dips.

"I will lead, Your Majesty. You will follow."

Now it's his turn to order.

Or perhaps I was kidding myself before.

Roc will never take commands. He *gives* them.

The assembled dancers fall into position around us, forming a loose circle in the center of the hall.

Roc holds up his hand and I slip mine into his and then the music is threading around us and Roc twirls me around and around until I'm dizzy, not just with the dance, but with his nearness, his scent, the weight of his hand at the small of my back, and the sure grip of his other as he steers me in the movements.

He is a skilled dancer. It doesn't matter if it's a reel, a waltz, or a landerwall. He knows them all and he is very, very good at them.

Everything Roc does he does with confidence.

I'm not sure he knows what it is to doubt himself.

Gods that must be freeing.

The band's tempo shifts, and our footwork is required to match the beat as all of us assembled follow the flowing movement of the circle.

Roc spins me, then pulls me back and the skirt of my dress blooms out like the petals of a buttercup.

"Why are you afraid?" His voice cuts in through the music, raspy at my ear.

"What do you mean?"

He spins me again as the dance requires, then pulls me back.

"You are afraid of something. Tell me what it is."

"You haven't earned my secrets."

He smiles and his arm shifts higher on my back so he can dip me in unison with the rest of the couples.

When he hoists me up, I'm dizzy with delight, but also on guard.

There is a look on his face like he's found something that he wants to claim and he will not stop until he has it.

"Tell me how to earn your secrets, Your Majesty."

"No."

"Why?"

"You abandoned me."

"Is that what you believe?"

With my hand firmly in his, I spin out to the center of the circle with all of the other women. And then Roc twirls me back in.

"I asked you to stay," he says. "You refused me."

"You cut off James's hand."

"If a hand touches what's mine, then the hand is mine too. And you were mine first." There is still a smile on his beautiful mouth, but the look in his eye has turned dark.

"I didn't belong to you."

He clucks his tongue. "Yes you did."

My insides clench at his words. I don't want to be a silly, simpering girl beneath Roc's attention and his assurances that I did in fact belong to him, but I'm not sure I can fight it, even all these years later.

But I'm not willing to give up just yet.

"And what about now?" I counter. "You and James?"

The darkness in his gaze lights like a bonfire. "Oh Wendy Darling, you haven't earned my secrets."

I scowl.

He turns me once, then twice as the song reaches its climax.

When he pulls me back into him, I careen with his hard chest and let out a huff while my entire body burns hot. There is no air between us now. Not an inch of open space.

A lock of Roc's dark hair falls over his forehead as the waltz crescendos. Our pace is fast now, the footwork complex, the spins and dips coming so quickly, the room blurs.

The violinist comes to a sudden halt, timed perfectly to us women spinning out from our partners, arms held aloft.

The crowd roars in delight, clapping and whistling.

I'm breathing heavily and a little sweaty. But Roc looks like he could dance another dozen waltzes.

"For someone who thinks she doesn't know how to dance, you did well."

I swallow and then words are tumbling out of my mouth. "Are you *with* him?"

Roc's green eyes burn like emeralds in the sun. "Oh, Your Majesty. Jealousy does not become you."

"I'm not jealous."

"No?"

"You took his hand!"

"Yes, everyone keeps reminding me of that."

"Are you playing games with him?"

He gets in close to me and says, "Are you?" I'm taken aback by the protective edge of his words as if I'm the one to watch out for.

My teeth grit together. I yank my hand out of his and leave the dance floor, excusing myself from the supper hall.

CHAPTER TWENTY-ONE
ROC

Wendy Darling thinks I abandoned her here?

I didn't even know she was in the Seven Isles until recently. Pan conveniently left out the detail where instead of taking her home to the mortal realm, he abandoned her on Everland.

If he wasn't a god, I would kill him just for the inconvenience.

Wendy darts from the hall, her dress billowing behind her, her heart thumping loudly even over the din of the court.

She's angry at me, yes, and now jealous that I have our lovely Captain and she doesn't. If she'd given me the opportunity, I would have told her there was more than enough room in my bed for her and the Captain. I can easily satisfy them both.

"Roc."

I hear the Captain calling my name.

I'm still locked on Wendy's disappearing figure.

The court has turned to the next song, a reel that's been out of fashion for some years now. I grab a glass from a passing server and take a long drink. Its champagne infused with berries. The bubbles pop on my tongue.

"Beast," the Captain hisses and I finally turn to him. "What did you say to her? Why did she run away?"

"She's jealous."

"Of what?"

"You and I."

He snorts. "There is no you and I."

I clutch at my heart. "You wound me, Captain."

"Oh don't be ridiculous."

I take another drink, emptying the champagne flute. I stalk the next closest server and switch out my glass.

"I'm going after her," the Captain says, starting for the door.

"To what end?"

"To see if she's all right."

I follow him from the hall. "She's not all right. She's mad, confused, and afraid of something. I wish she'd tell me what so I can kill it and we can be done with this."

The Captain lowers his voice, leaning into me, but it still sounds like he's shouting at me. "You can't go around threatening to kill someone in a foreign court!"

"Now who's being ridiculous? Of course I can."

"The fact that you never concern yourself with consequences—"

"Is impressive?" I cut in.

"No." His scowl deepens. "Worrisome."

"Ahh. That was going to be my seventh guess."

He gives me another look, clearly vexed with me and it makes me want to poke and prod at him more.

An annoyed Captain makes me hungry.

We stop in the middle of the arched hallway. A few courtesans amble past, but everyone steers clear of me.

"How about this? You go after our dearest Darling," I tell him. "And I'll go in search of information."

"What kind of information and in what way? No stabbing or killing."

"Are you giving me orders?"

"If I were, would you abide them?"

I shrug and scan the hall. "If you ordered me to please you, I would."

He screws up his mouth. "Well I would never."

His heart ticks up a beat, telling me he's lying.

"Sure sure," I say. "Now run along, Captain. I have work to do."

With a huff, he disappears down the hall leaving me to my own devices.

IT'S MY OPINION THAT IF YOU WANT INFORMATION, YOU ASK THE help.

The help can get into places that regular people can't and often they're overlooked, so they hear things that no one else hears.

I start with the kitchen staff.

The page is so distracted he barely gives me a second glance so I don't bother with him. There's a line cook in the kitchen pouring boiling water down a drain. Her face is red and splotchy like the night has gotten the best of her. Not quite what I'm looking for.

I find a young woman in the scullery scrubbing dried onion soup from serving bowls. She's hunched over the stone trough sink, bubbles and dishes up to her elbows.

Leaning against the doorway, I say, "I find the work goes faster if you just toss the dishes into the trash."

She startles at the sound of my voice and then hastens to bow.

I guess my reputation has found its way here already, to this dark corner of the kitchen.

"Can I help you, sir?" she asks, head bent, eyes downcast.

"Something is troubling me."

"If I can help, sir, I will try."

She has the soft, olive complexion of the Summerlanders, and the thick, curly hair too. If that didn't give it away, her accent would. It's a lilting accent with a soft trill on the Rs.

"I was just in the supper hall," I start, "and someone told me I should be careful around here? You'll have to forgive me, it's been so long since I've been on Everland soil. You wouldn't happen to know what they were talking about, would you?" I take a step into the scullery. "I don't want to find myself in a spot of trouble, you know."

"Of course not, sir." Her wet hands twist up in the ivory apron tied around her waist. "But it's not really my place to talk."

I make a *tsk-tsk* with my tongue and her eyes catch on my mouth, the way my lips form the sound.

Her olive complexion floods with rose.

I know what I do to women. It's a gift and a curse. More gift than curse if I'm honest. I don't know that my dashing good looks and relentless charm has ever gotten me into trouble.

It's definitely gotten me out of it on more than one occasion.

I take another step. The girl tries to fill her lungs, but I can hear the shallowness of the breath and the rapid thump-thump of her heart. She knows me, of course, they all know me. And getting cornered in a scullery with a beast such as myself can either be the preamble to a good time or a very bad one.

But I have no designs on the girl. I just want the information.

"If I promise to keep it between us," I say, lowering my voice to a husky rumble, "would that help loosen your tongue?"

At the word *tongue*, she gulps down another breath.

"I shouldn't—"

I didn't think it would take quite this much maneuvering, but just as well I suppose.

I pull a fairy bar from my pocket and toss it to her. She catches it, but her slippery hands lose it and the bar clings loudly against the stone floor.

When she spots exactly what it is, her eyes get big and round like full moons and then she's tripping over her words.

"I don't mean to...or perhaps...you must know...ahhh..." She eyes the bar again. She hasn't budged to snatch it. "Sir," she tries again.

"Pick up the bar." My voice is level, not at all threatening. But she chokes on a breath and then stoops down for the gold. It quickly disappears into the pocket of her apron.

"You were saying?" I push.

She wrings her hands. "Promise you won't tell on me for gossiping?"

I lift my little finger. "It's a pinky promise."

She smiles nervously, then hooks her pinky around mine. The heat that rises in her neck turns her skin bright red.

"Go on then. We are now bound by oath."

This brightens her eyes.

"Well..." Her gaze darts over my shoulder as if she's looking for eavesdroppers. But my hearing is better than her vision and I don't detect anyone within twenty feet and those in the kitchen are too busy buzzing around cleaning up after the five-course meal.

"There are rumors about a witch infiltrating the court."

"No!" I say, aghast.

"Yes. The king and the prince do not age, you see. And it all started with the arrival of the new queen, Queen Wendellyn."

Wendy changed her name?

"Then what?"

The girl leans in. We're co-conspirators now and we're having a hell of a good time.

"First the king stopped aging."

"Shut up," I say.

"Truly! And that was right after he married his new queen. Then his son, the prince, over the next several years, he too stopped aging and there were rumors that the queen was having an illicit affair with the prince."

"Scandalous."

"I know!" The girl covers her mouth as a giggle bursts from her throat.

I don't like that she's reveling in the supposed wicked affairs of Wendy, but when one is gathering information, one must act the part.

"What else?" I ask.

"Well, early this year, the king stopped appearing in public and they say he's now dying, having aged rapidly over night and he's now slipped into a coma."

"So we think the queen has turned on him?"

The girl nods.

"Why? What would she stand to gain? She'll lose her throne when he dies."

The girl's eyes gleam.

"Oh you have more? Do tell."

"Well." She checks the doorway again, and then plunges on. "Years back, the king amended the royal code and instead of the prince inheriting the throne on his father's death, Queen Wendellyn will."

Well I didn't expect that.

"Why would he do that?"

The girl shrugs. "Maybe she twisted his mind into doing it with her dark magic."

I was raised steeped in darkness. I know dark power when I see it and when Wendy Darling was brought to Neverland all those years ago, she had no power to speak of.

But when she dragged us into the castle this morning, I did sense something different about her.

It's not often a mortal *becomes* magical, but the Seven Isles are full of tricks.

The girl goes on, but she's just tossing out her own theories now. Maybe Wendy is secretly a dark fae (she's not). Maybe she has designs to kill the king and marry the prince (she'll marry that shit over my dead body). Maybe she's a fairy godmother come to punish a wicked court (wouldn't that be hilarious).

I stop listening at fairy godmother (no fairy godmothers reside in this realm) when my hearing picks up on a steady beating heart just outside the scullery.

Someone is listening.

The breathing is just as steady as the heart beat. This someone is no stranger to eavesdropping. They aren't nervous about getting caught. An interesting position to have when you're eavesdropping on a beast.

By the tempo of the heart rate, I'm guessing it's a woman.

I let the scullery maid drone on as I take a few silent steps toward the doorway.

And then—

I pop out into the hallway.

There's no one there.

"Is something the matter?" the girl asks.

I turn back to her and smile. "You've been extremely helpful. I shouldn't keep you from your work any longer."

She glances at the full trough sink and frowns. "Yes, I suppose you're right."

"Could you do me a favor and not mention my visit?"

The girl blushes harder. "Of course, Mr. Crocodile."

See? Of course she knows me.

I take her hand in mine and kiss her wet knuckles. She catches herself on the edge of the sink as her knees wobble from what I can only presume is equal parts fright and elation.

"Good night, *petit pois*," I whisper.

She lets out a little huff of air. "Good night, sir."

CHAPTER TWENTY-TWO
ROC

I wouldn't call slipping into the king's bedroom an easy feat, but I manage to bribe one of the nurses with my charm and wit and some of the Captain's silver. I'm curious about the king, but I'm not curious enough to hand over a fairy bar. My reserves are dwindling and my cache is in a Darkland bank, so I must be selective in my spending.

The darkness in the king's room is no enemy of mine, but the stench certainly is. I can smell decaying flesh on the air and the rot of magic.

This entire situation is getting more and more interesting by the second.

At the old man's bedside, I watch him breathe.

His lungs rattle like a Summerland cicada and his mouth is gaping open like a fish.

"Well you are most certainly dying, aren't you? Do you know how much trouble you're causing with your inferior mortal body?"

I bend closer, listening for any change in heart rate or breathing to tell me whether or not he's conscious of my presence.

His patterns remain.

I rip the blanket from his body.

He's just skin and bones, and barely skin he's so pale and old.

A shiver runs through me.

Mortality is unfortunate and I'm glad I don't suffer from its consequences.

There's nothing about the king's body that gives me pause. Everything is as it should be for an old dying man.

But still, the reek of magic is there, a scent that I am all too familiar with.

I check the bedside table, the candle burning in its bronze holder, the glass bottles of medicine. Nothing is amiss.

So where is it? Where is the magic coming from?

I take a few steps back and then it comes to me.

The bed.

It's large, practically an island on its own. Four posters with a thick canopy.

Grabbing it by the post near the king's head, I give it a yank. The monstrosity moves a few inches and the rug bunches up beneath my feet.

Another yank and there is enough dead space for me to stick my head around the backside, between the bed and the wall.

And there...

There's where I find it.

A maker's mark.

A circle with two wings and two intertwined Ms.

The Myth Makers.

"Well fuck me," I say on a breath.

Growing up in a secret society had its perks. More for myself than for Vane, who tried to shed the benefits like an insufferable cloak. My baby brother is stubborn like that. And truth be told, he would much rather take a thing than be handed it.

I do admire that about him. Even if I can't understand it.

The Bone Society and The Myth Makers have, for most of our history, been allies. But that's because we don't get in the way of the Myths and they don't get in ours.

But twice now, on two different islands, I've found them meddling, *expanding*, putting their fingers into things they should not be putting their fingers in.

I shove the bed back into place and make sure to straighten the rug. Then I tuck the dusty king back into his blanket.

There is no saving the man now. No magic, no miracle will bring his corpse back to life. Because I'd put the rest of my fairy gold on the fact that him lying on death's door has the Myths' fingerprints all over it.

The only thing to be done now is to rescue Wendy from whatever dark, twisted plot the Myth Makers have running through the Everland Court.

Sooner rather than later.

But first, I need a fucking shower to scrub the stench of death from my skin. Maybe a distraction or two to clear my head.

Then we get to work.

CHAPTER TWENTY-THREE

HOOK

I'M NO STRANGER TO ROYAL HOUSES, BUT THIS CASTLE IS A labyrinth and though I have no watch to consult, I suspect I've been wandering for half of an hour, maybe more.

Where the bloody hell is Wendy?

I've turned down a darker hall where the flame in the gas sconces on the walls flicker a little lower. I may have wandered into a wing of the castle not meant for me but I'm determined now. I don't want to meet up with the Crocodile again with having made little progress in our mission.

My footsteps are quiet as I follow the plush rug that runs down the center of the hall so it's easy to catch the hushed tones of a secret conversation happening just beyond a cracked doorway to my left.

I check behind me to make sure I'm alone. The hall is empty.

I press my shoulder into the wall and lean as close to the open doorway as I dare. Eavesdropping is poor form but I'm convincing myself it's worth it if it helps Wendy.

But the voice I catch isn't her. It's the prince's betrothed.

What is she saying?

"You should have consulted with me before inviting the queen's friends to dinner."

The voice that responds is the nasally tone of the prince.

"I shouldn't have to ask for your permission."

"Yes but we are in this together, are we not?"

He grunts. "Of course we are."

"Then decisions must be made together and inviting them has endangered everything."

Am I hearing this correctly?

It's easy to convince yourself that you've misheard something when you're practically hunched over, straining your hearing, trying to catch every syllable and only getting half.

When I first crossed paths with the prince and his betrothed, I didn't take her for a forthright sort of woman. She seemed shy and skittish, as if the pop of a balloon might startle her.

Clearly I misread her. Either that, or she misrepresented herself. Which begs the question: *why*?

I scavenge through my memories for her place in them and come up blank again. I swear I've met her before.

What exactly does she think the Crocodile and I are endangering?

Roc's words about Wendy echo in my head: *She's mad, confused, and afraid of something.*

Is it the prince and his soon-to-be bride? Every court has a warring heir and stepparent so I wouldn't be surprised. But the thought of Wendy being in danger because of a scheming prince has my blood pumping.

I still my breathing to hear anything else that might be pertinent.

The prince says, "What would you like me to do with them, then?"

The girl is silent a moment, and then she says, "You keep your attention on your dying father. Leave the queen's guests to me."

Bloody hell.

I turn away from the door and run from the hall.

What have we walked into the middle of?

CHAPTER TWENTY-FOUR

HOOK

I barge into the Crocodile's room unannounced and when he comes out of the washroom soaking wet, a towel wrapped around his waist, I silently chastise myself for not, at the very least, *knocking*.

All of the things I wanted to tell him, the things I overheard, are suddenly gone from my mind.

He is the distraction I don't need and now all of the alarm bells that were ringing in my head are silent, when they should be ringing louder.

There is only the sizzling warmth, like bottled lightning, running from my throat, down my stomach, down to my cock.

Water droplets collect on his skin skimming over the dark ink that decorates his chest. There are a riot of flowers and vines, with a name in script in the center. *Lainey*, it says. His sister.

I never would have taken the Crocodile for a sentimental man, but the ink has me questioning that assumption. And didn't he return to Neverland for his brother?

He likes to pretend he loves nothing, but I think he's lying.

I think he loves people from a distance so that if they manage to break his heart, they're too far away to notice.

More water drips down the flat plane of his stomach, following the trail of dark hair that disappears beneath the low hanging towel.

I get a flash of my cock in his mouth and in an instant, I'm straining against my pants.

When I finally drag my eyes away from his body and back to his face, I find him starting at me, amusement in his green eyes.

"Captain," he says and then makes his way past me to the bar to pour himself a few fingers of brandy. "Did you only come here to gape at me or did you want something?"

"Apologies." Heat flames in my face. "Your door was unlocked."

"So it was." He turns to me, slings back the drink, his eyes on me the entire time.

Tension practically vibrates between us.

I fight the urge to readjust my cock.

He's going to notice eventually.

I need to get the hell out of here.

But didn't I come here for a reason?

Right.

"I thought you might want to know what I overheard between the prince and his betrothed."

"I'm listening," he says as he pours himself another drink.

I tell him all. And when I'm finished, his gaze is unfocused as if lost in deep thought.

"So?" I coax.

"So?" His dark brow rises. "It's interesting."

"Interesting? It's suspicious at the very least."

"Yes." He refills his glass for a third time, but now there are two. He hands me the second glass, his lower half still wrapped in a towel.

"Shouldn't you get dressed?"

"Should I?"

"Yes," I tell him. "It's poor form."

"Is it?"

I huff out and sip from my brandy trying to do anything other than look at him.

"Very well," he says and then removes the towel and there is no force in the world that could have kept my eyes from looking down.

Bloody hell.

Like every part of him, he's perfect.

I can imagine him using that cock on me and the thought sends blood rushing to my balls.

"Captain," he says again and I have to drag my eyes away from his crotch.

I clear my throat. "Why are you toying with me?" The question was meant to sound accusatory, but instead it comes out sounding like a plea.

"If there was any part of you that didn't want to be toyed with, it wouldn't be so fucking easy. Now would it?"

He sounds angry now so I scowl at him, matching his ire. "We're here for Wendy."

"Yes."

"We are not here for one another."

"Aren't we?"

"No."

"Tell that to the bulge between your legs."

I suck in a breath through my nose, nostrils flaring. The anger is tenfold now, because he's dissected me so easily, because there is nowhere to hide when standing in front of an immortal beast.

I should leave. I know I should. There is a body part literally missing because of him. Every part of my rational brain is yelling at me to go, but the primal side, the disastrous side, the empty, hungry, desolate side, can never seem to walk away from him.

Can't my revenge be in taking pleasure from him instead? Let the feel of his touch replace the memory of his pain?

He empties his glass and his cock twitches as I watch him.

Perhaps the greater revenge is in seeing the Crocodile come undone because of me.

I suddenly want nothing more than to hear him come, to hear his grunts, feel his hips grinding against me. I want that arrogant prick to find himself desperate for me.

He must read the look on my face because he gestures behind me with a flick of his finger and says, "Close the door, Captain."

This is the moment I can escape if I really want to. Prove to him and to me that I won't fall for his games.

But I can't escape. I can't run. I know I can't because I don't want to.

I want to keep playing this game with him and see if I may emerge the victor.

I want to hold something over him.

I take three steps to the door and shove it closed.

When I turn around, the Crocodile is there, having crossed the room on silent, bare feet. "That's a good boy," he tells me, and then his mouth is crashing into mine.

I backpedal, surprised, and slam into the door. His hand comes around my throat, fingers pressing against the sharp line of my jaw, directing our kiss with the kind of demand only an immortal beast can possess.

He could devour me whole if he wanted to, and I think I'd let him.

The line of his body against mine is hard and domineering and I feel the press of his hardening cock against my thigh.

Heat races up my spine. He is a razor blade dragged across my skin, and I am testing his sharpness.

Will he cut me? Do I even care anymore? I will bleed black if he does. Every second I am with him, I am courting darkness. His, mine, there is no longer a difference.

My father would hate everything about the man I've become.

Poor form indeed.

I reach between us as the Crocodile tastes the brandy on my tongue and grab hold of his shaft.

He groans into my mouth and the sound is like a symphony to my ears.

There is no greater sound.

Nothing on this fucking earth.

I squeeze him at the base, then stroke downward, bringing my thumb over his wet slit.

He breaks the kiss, grabs my hand and shoves my thumb into my mouth so I can taste him.

He's salty and sharp.

His green eyes flash yellow and goosebumps roll up my arms.

Then he's yanking my clothes off, frenzied, ravenous and I'm on that heaving wave again, the rest of the world a dark smudge around me.

He yanks me to the bed, tosses me back and I have just enough time to pull myself up against the pillows before he's on me, his mouth on my neck, nipping at my skin, our cocks hard and hot against one another.

I arch my back trying to get closer to him, put he pushes forward with his hips, pinning me down.

A useless gasp escapes me.

I will drown here with him.

I *am* drowning.

He reaches between us, teasing my ass with the brush of his fingers and it takes everything in me not to blow right then and there.

I widen my eyes, focus on the slight shift of the canopy above us as a breeze steals in through the drafty castle windows.

If I come right now, it will be over too soon and I will be left wishing for more.

"Wait," I tell him.

He sits back on his knees.

"I feel like I'm losing my fucking mind," I confess.

"I have that affect on people."

"Shut up," I tell him and he presses his lips together but smiles at me in a way that suggests he knows just how to brag with his eyes.

"Promise me you won't bite."

"I promise," he says easily as if our entire history hasn't been established on the fact that we like to hurt one another.

"Go slow," I warn him.

"I know how to fuck a tight ass, Captain."

He leans over me, reaching into the small drawer of the bedside table. As he does, his cock presses into me and a burning, raging desire has me gasping out a breath.

I lift my hips and fist us both and the Crocodile hisses in response.

He freezes halfway over top of me, his hands still in the bedside table.

"Keep going," he tells me, his voice a deep rasp.

I jerk us both and his dick swells in my grip as he huffs out a desperate breath.

He grabs whatever item he needed and repositions over top of me, his elbows on either side of my head. He rocks his hips forward, seeking my touch.

"You keep doing that, Captain," he says, "and I will be blowing in your hand before I have a chance at your ass."

My own touch pales in comparison to his, but there is something carnal about grinding against him, steely flesh against steely flesh.

"Is that what you want?" I ask him. "To have all of me?"

I don't want to sound so needy, but there is nothing I want more than to hear him admit to his desire.

"Yes," he says.

"Then do it."

He leans back on his knees. There is a glass bottle in his hands and he uncorks it, filling the other palm with a clear, slippery liquid.

"Do you bring lube with you everywhere you go?"

Recorking it, he tosses the bottle. It thuds to the floor.

Then he clamps his clean hand over my mouth. My startled breath huffs out.

His green eyes meet mine and flare yellow. "It's your turn to shut the fuck up." He's serious now, his voice deep and raspy. "You get six words. *More. Harder. Stop. Slower. God. Fuck.* Now stop being so difficult and let me take care of you. All right?"

In my head, I am watching an ocean wave rise up, blotting out the sun.

He waits for my answer.

I finally give him a nod of acknowledgment.

"Good," he says and then strokes himself with the lube, leaving his cock wet and glistening.

Then he flips me over onto my stomach and I clutch at the twisted blanket losing myself in the sway of the wave as the Crocodile, my mortal enemy, presses his cock into my ass.

CHAPTER TWENTY-FIVE
WENDY

Asha finds me hiding in my secret room. Its doorway is tucked behind a bookcase in one of the rarely used sitting rooms on the third floor. Hald gave it to me when I first came to the castle and realized I had no love for court drama and politics.

Sometimes I just need to hide.

And right now, I wish I could crawl into the shadows and never come out.

"I've been looking for you," Asha says.

I've shed the dress and am now in a nightgown and silk robe with the Grimmaldi crest stitched in gold on the back. There is a log crackling on the hearth. When Hald showed me the room, he taught me how to start a fire too.

I tip my glass, half full of spiced wine, at Asha. "You've found me."

Asha wasn't at the supper tonight. She was on duty on the curtain wall. Or at least she was supposed to be. But now looking over her clothes, I have to wonder if she dodged her duties and went on a discovery mission.

She's not wearing the soldier's typical on-duty uniform,

that of a single breasted short tailed coat with gold aiguil-lettes and cotton trousers.

Instead, she's entirely done in black: black form-fitting coat and black leather breeches with supple black leather boots. Her dark hair is braided in a tight Winterland braid.

"The Crocodile was in the kitchen tonight asking questions."

I sit upright. "Did he see you?"

Asha clasps her hands behind her back and straightens her shoulders. "Of course not."

That's just what I need, Roc going after my best friend, my only ally.

"What was he asking?"

"Too many questions," she says.

Of course he was.

"Did he get any answers?"

She nods, rather grimly.

Great.

I set the glass aside and stand up. I was on my third glass and I wish I could say it's made me tipsy, but it's only made me more melancholy. There is nothing to do in this court other than drink and eat.

"Let me handle him." I start for the door.

"Wendy."

I stop, hand on the door lever.

"I've asked you to consider an escape plan for months and you've come up with excuses every single time. I'm not taking no for an answer now. The risks are too high."

Closing my eyes, I exhale, promising my turning and twisting stomach that someday, things will be better, that I won't have to feel this constant pit of anxiety, this incessant pulse of fear.

"I made Hald a promise."

"You shouldn't have to risk your life and your safety for a promise."

I think she might be right, but in the years since Pan dropped me here, Everland has become my home. Or at least as close to home as a foreign land can be. If I don't have Everland, then what is left?

A voice whispers in the deep, dark recesses of my mind: *you have Roc and James.*

When I accused Roc of abandoning me, he seemed surprised by it, almost offended.

Did Peter Pan tell them I never made it home? What about Smee? My time with her was always urgent and short. I was focused on getting my baby out of Everland and to safety, far, far away from Peter Pan and the Seven Isles.

I assumed she told James where I was, and that if James knew, then so did Roc.

I never stopped to ask myself what Smee would have gained by sharing my whereabouts. Nothing. She would have gained absolutely nothing. Instead, she would have risked James's life at a time when he was already defeated.

Maybe this entire time, I've been blaming the wrong people for my fate.

Perhaps it's time I faced Roc and James and found out what truly brought them here.

CHAPTER TWENTY-SIX

WENDY

I TRY JAMES'S DOOR FIRST, RAPPING SOFTLY AGAINST THE WOOD, but there is no sound on the other side and when I poke my head in, I find the room empty.

Where is he?

I glance down the hall to Roc's room where the door is shut.

I go there, but before I can knock, I catch the sound of faint grunting and my heart catches in my throat.

What if Hally has already gotten to them? What if he's trying to hurt them right now?

I burst into the room and—

I suck in a breath.

The blood freezes in my veins.

"Oh god." I stumble back. "I—I...I shouldn't...*oh god*."

They are on the bed, *together*, sweat coating their skin.

My mind immediately goes to embarrassment and my body immediately goes to exhilaration.

This is something I shouldn't be seeing and yet...and yet...I can't tear my eyes away.

"Does no one know how to knock?" Roc says.

I turn for the door, but Roc is suddenly there, slamming it shut.

"You have two choices," he tells me, his hair damp and mussed, his lips red and swollen, his cock soaking wet.

My pussy clenches at the sight of him. It remembers quite well what it was to be fucked by him. I never would have thought I'd be jealous of James getting that part of Roc. I thought they hated each other more than anything else in the world.

"One," Roc says, "you come over to the bed and you join us."

My mouth drops open.

"Two, you sit in that chair and you watch."

Sense comes back to me like a slow trickle of water. I cross my arms over my chest realizing that I've barged into his room in nothing but my nightclothes.

"Or how about the third option?" I challenge. "I leave."

Roc surrounds me and I backpedal into the door. He puts his hand on it just above my head, caging me in on one side. Every hard line of him is in my face, overwhelming me. On the surface, there is nothing to differentiate Roc from any other man, but deep down my body knows that he is danger personified, more monster than man.

The hair rises along my neck.

"Do you want to leave, Your Majesty?" he asks me.

I start to answer, try to form the three letters into one word—*yes*—but it won't come out. Because the letters are actually wrong, because the answer is *no*.

My silence says everything.

"Then I repeat," Roc says, "you have two choices."

"Crocodile," James says, nearly a hiss.

But Roc cuts him with a look over his shoulder and says, "Six words, Captain. Remember?"

James falls quiet, scowling at Roc.

What does 'six words' mean? It's things like this that remind me of just how outside of them I am. They have coded language, secrets, and inside jokes.

How long have they been together? How did it even happen?

Are they *together*-together?

"I'm married," I tell Roc.

"I won't hold it against you," he says.

I shouldn't be here. I shouldn't be doing this. Not because I'm married. Hald has had so many mistresses in the time of our marriage, I've lost count. In fact, he encouraged me to take on a lover several times before.

It's not Hald and any duty to the marriage.

It's Roc and James.

It's the temptation of them.

It's the terror that they'll leave me again as they did before and I will be left clinging to the memory of them, scrambling for scraps of a life.

If they're together, they don't need me.

I tilt my chin, looking up at Roc. "Did you know I was here? Did either of you know?"

"No, we didn't," Roc confirms.

I look between him and James. "Then why now? Why did you come?"

Roc's answer is quick. "For you."

"Why?"

James climbs off the bed and comes over. He too is naked, his cock so hard, it's pointing at me, the tip glistening.

I swallow, my body buzzing in a way it hasn't buzzed since I left Neverland.

I expect James to give me an explanation, something to help it all make sense.

But instead, he takes a chunk of my hair in hand, yanks my head back and kisses me.

All of the tension melts from my body.

James kisses like he didn't know what it was to breathe until our mouths were meeting.

A shiver races up my spine.

He kisses me long and deep and the air is warm against my skin, his lips warmer still.

And when he breaks it, he rests his forehead against mine and says, "I've missed you all of the days that have stretched between then and now. If I'd known you were here, pregnant with my baby, I would have come, Wendy Darling. I would have saved you or died trying."

Tears burn in my eyes and my chin wobbles, but James holds fast. He gives me the intensity of his stare so I know...*I know*...that he is telling the truth.

I break down. Right there in his arms. I sob like no time at all has passed, like I'm still the girl in that dark, wet prison cell, watching my belly grow, knowing that no one is coming to save me.

But every day I dreamed of it. Of James or Roc or both sweeping in through that prison door and taking me far, far away.

"I'm sorry we didn't come," James tells me. "But we are here now."

I nod against him and then our mouths crash together. He drives me back against the wall. Our kisses are frenzied, hungry, desperate to close the distance between all the years hanging between us.

He unties my robe, yanks it from my body, then wraps

his hand and his hook around my thighs, hoisting me up into his arms.

We bang against the wall. The thin straps of my nightgown slip from my shoulders and my breasts hit the air, nipples peaking. James takes one in his mouth, his tongue sliding over the tight bud and I arch my back, eager for more of him.

I know I shouldn't be here. I know I shouldn't be doing this.

But I am lost in him, in the desperation to feel saved.

And when my eyes drift open, refocus, I spot Roc behind us, watching.

I hold out my hand for him, panting, as James uses his hook to tear off my panties.

My pussy is throbbing, dripping wet. To have them both, at the same time...it's so illicit, so wrong...

I haven't been this turned on in...forever.

"Please," I beg Roc.

It isn't until James glances back and gives Roc a nod that he comes.

"Hold on to me, Wendy," James says.

I wind my arms around his neck, holding on tight as he lines himself up at my opening.

Roc puts his mouth to James's ear. "Don't go easy on her, Captain."

James's gaze darkens. His hook digs into the back of my thigh and pain bites into my skin.

"I would suspect the queen needs to be properly fucked," Roc adds and then, taking Roc's orders, James plunges hard inside of me.

CHAPTER TWENTY-SEVEN
ROC

I'VE HAD PLENTY OF THREESOMES. SEVERAL FOURSOMES. SOME fivesomes.

But this is different.

Everything about this is different.

I like watching them.

I'm usually the one starring in the show.

I'm hardly ever the audience.

And yet I can't tear my eyes away from them. From the way Wendy's mouth drops open, forming an O, her adorable little gasps of ecstasy making her squeak.

The way the Captain holds on to her tightly, spoiling her with his attention, thrusting into her like her pussy is made of stars and magic.

My stomach rolls, cock twitching.

I give them a few more minutes alone, give myself a few more minutes to gorge myself on the sight of them, and then I'm grabbing the bottle of lube, prepping my cock again.

I want to join their pleasure and drench myself in it.

I stroke my cock from base to head until it's rock hard and soaked.

I get in behind the Captain and as soon as he senses the heat of my cock, he slows his thrusting, widening his stance to give me his ass.

I'm so eager to stretch him open again, pre-cum is already beading at the tip. The Captain and I weren't able to finish. Not before Wendy Darling burst into my room.

Perfect fucking timing. Because now I get to watch her come while the Captain comes, while his ass tightens around me and I fill him up.

Over his shoulder, Wendy meets my eyes.

There is a warning there.

Do not hurt him.

The Captain pushes his hips forward, fucking Wendy with a hard thrust. And when he rocks back, pulling out of her, I sink in.

He huffs out a startled breath and collapses into Wendy. She readjusts, one arm around his neck, her other hand on my shoulder, bracing herself.

The Captain's hole takes half of me and his tight ass is fucking nirvana.

Why did I ever hate him? It makes no sense now. I could have been fucking him this entire time. I could have made him mine.

Wendy's eyes slip closed. The Captain pumps into her, every one of his movements a back-and-forth dance. Fuck Wendy, rock back, fuck me.

"Oh my god," Wendy breathes out. "I can't believe we're doing this."

I push two of my fingers into the Captain's mouth and he takes me eagerly, swirling his tongue around me.

When I pop them back out again, I sink the wetness to Wendy's clit.

She moans, long and loudly, her fingers tightening on my bare shoulder.

"I'm close," she warns.

"Me too," the Captain says.

"I want to hear you both come," I order them. "Let me feel your pleasure."

The Captain's pace picks up and Wendy's body knocks against the wall with every one of his thrusts and every time he pulls out of her, he takes me closer and closer to my own edge.

I swirl my two fingers around Wendy's clit and her body tightens up, her breathing shallower.

"Oh fuck. Oh...fuck," she says and then she's shouting through the orgasm, her body writhing against the wall.

The muscle in the Captain's shoulders dimples as his own body tenses up, giving and taking.

He grunts into her and I match his pace, finding the rhythm I want.

And when he spills inside of her, his breathing heavy and stilted, there is nothing in the world that could stop me from joining him.

I'm so fucking ready to fill him up.

One hand wrapped around his throat, the other on his hip, I drive into his tight, wet ass and spill a load so fucking big, it'll be dripping out of him for days.

The Captain trembles beneath me, goosebumps popping along his shoulders despite the sweat coating his skin.

Wendy's eyes slip closed as she loses herself to the aftershocks of her pleasure.

And I bear witness to them both, to their ecstasy, their pleasure.

I don't think I've ever seen something so fucking beautiful.

CHAPTER TWENTY-EIGHT
HOOK

WENDY'S LEGS TREMBLE AS I LET HER GO AND SHE SLUMPS AGAINST the wall. Roc steps in, collecting her in his arms and carrying her to his bed. I go to the washroom and get a warm, wet cloth.

With my hook, I nudge her knees apart and her eyes open to slits, watching me as I clean her.

I wasn't there when she was abandoned, and all through her pregnancy and while giving birth. I can't imagine the pain and horror of doing all of it alone and I'm overcome with the need to take care of her now and forever.

Within minutes, she's fast asleep, curled on her side, her arm tucked beneath the Crocodile's pillow.

It wouldn't surprise me if she rarely sleeps in this treacherous place.

Still naked and not at all bothered by it, the Crocodile pours us each a drink, then collapses into the chair. He lights a cigarette and as he inhales on it, the crocodile mouth tattooed along his neck moves.

I sit in the matching chair beside him.

The room is dark and quiet save for Wendy's soft breaths and Roc's exhale of smoke.

We watch her for several long minutes. She does not stir.

I wonder if he too thinks she's an aberration. If we blink, if she will disappear again.

I nurse my brandy.

Roc downs his.

The tobacco crackles when he takes another hit.

"Can I confess something?" he finally says, his voice low so as not to disturb Wendy.

To have a secret belonging to the Crocodile must be akin to possessing a rare jewel. I'm suddenly eager for it.

"Go for it," I tell him pretending that I don't care when really my heart is beating so fast, I can feel it on the back of my tongue.

His head shifts against the velvet fabric of his chair. I hear the rasp of his thick hair against it, hear the intake of breath as he looks at me and says, "Taking your hand is my greatest regret."

I frown at him.

I'm not sure what I expected him to say but it isn't this. And certainly not in this way. His voice husky, his gaze heavy, like what he's said actually matters to him.

The Crocodile is so rarely serious that it takes me by surprise.

"I want to believe you," I say, "but lies so easily spill from your tongue."

His mouth lifts in a half smile. "Perhaps I will tell you one more then." He pauses. "I loathe you, Captain. Every fucking inch."

Everything the Crocodile says is a puzzle, something to

be turned over and scrutinized. But I think this might be the most honest things he's ever told me.

Truth wrapped up in a lie so as to hide just how vulnerable it is.

The thought of the Crocodile, the Devourer of Men, desiring me, *every fucking inch*, makes me feel like a fucking king.

"Why did you take my hand then?" I lift my hook, gesturing at him. "I mean, I know she is your excuse." I nod at the line of Wendy's body tucked beneath the blanket. "But why, exactly? You had no claim to her. And you yourself have admitted you don't feel love."

He considers my question for a long time. I take another drink from my glass relishing the burn of the liquor, wishing it was rum instead.

"That's another lie," he admits. "I *am* capable of love. But everything I have ever loved has left me."

His words are barely more than a breath, edged in heartbreak.

My eyes turn glassy, but I sniff back the tears. I don't know if he wants my sympathy. I'm not even sure I'm ready to give it to him. "That can't be true," I say.

"Do not contradict my own confessions."

I sit forward so I can see him better around the wings of the chairs. "You were afraid she would leave you for me."

"Yes," he admits. "And when I am afraid, I do not think. I *act*."

"And instead, she left us both."

He laughs. "She showed us, didn't she?"

Our attention strays back to her. "I want to be angry at Peter Pan for abandoning her here, but if he hadn't, she would have returned to the mortal realm and she would long be dead."

"Yes." Roc drains his glass and sets it aside. "But we can still hate him for it, that ungodly prick."

I laugh too. "I suppose we can."

He finishes his cigarette next and drops it into the empty glass where it sizzles in the dregs of his brandy.

"It begs the question though," I go on, "why is she still alive? The Seven Isles are not the mortal realm, of course, but Everland has never been known to sustain aging quite like Neverland. She should also be dead here. She's not immortal. And yet she hasn't aged a day."

"About that."

I cut my gaze to him. "You know something?"

"Apparently, there are rumors swirling around the court that she's a witch. That when she married the king, he too stopped aging."

"When did you hear that?"

"Tonight, in the kitchen."

I scoff. "You have to fuck that secret out of the staff too?"

"Do I belong to you now, Captain?"

"Excuse me?"

"Well you're acting like a possessive *par amour* so I just want to be sure I know the state of things."

"I'm not your lover." Except there is a churning in my gut that feels an awful lot like betrayal, as if he is, as if he belongs to me.

Goddammit. Goddamn him.

But in the eyes of Commander William H. Hook, having a partner such as the Crocodile is no greater example of *poor form*.

He has no morals, no loyalty, no ambition. He is everything my father hated in a man.

I know what he would say if he saw me now with Roc: *you are a stain on the name Hook.*

I surge to my feet. "I need some air."

"Captain," Roc says, almost a growl. "I didn't fuck the kitchen staff. In fact, I didn't fuck the girl from the tavern either. I was just..." He sighs.

"It's fine. I don't care if you did." Yes I do. "I'll be back. Just...watch her."

I'm at the door in an instant, but he surges to his feet and stops me there, a cold hand on my wrist. I don't know that I like how he can move so quickly without a sound. It's a reminder that he isn't human. A reminder that I *am*.

"Be careful," he warns. It's impossible not to hear the thread of worry in his voice and my gut clenches.

I give him a nod. "I will."

CHAPTER TWENTY-NINE
WENDY

THERE IS ONLY COLD AND DARKNESS.

And everywhere I look, there is nothing but more of it.

Slowly it closes in, threatening to swallow me whole.

Then I'm sobbing and shivering as I'm escorted to the gallows where a rope is tied around my neck.

They pull the lever. The trapdoor drops. I'm weightless for one second and then the rope snaps.

I lurch awake covered in a cold sweat.

I don't recognize my surroundings but at least I'm not in the prison cell.

"What was the dream?"

Roc's voice finds me from the shadows. The drapes are closed, the lights turned down. An oil lantern flickers on the dresser casting deep shadows over his silhouette.

I pull myself against the headboard and kick off the sheet. I'm in my nightgown, but it's twisted around my legs and damp around my chest.

The discomfort of being sticky, exhausted, and disoriented is something I'm used to by now, but I still hate it.

"What was the dream?" Roc asks again.

I scrub at my face. "The usual stuff."

He sits forward, elbows on his knees, and the light catches him, washing him in sharp gold.

The effect of him emerging from the shadows, all of his pale and dark beauty, startles me and a hard breath zings down my throat.

When I was on Neverland, I would have done anything for his attention. I was obsessed with him. I had never met anyone like him. At times, he is so casual, so easygoing, that it's easy to drop your guard, forgetting that beneath the charm and good looks, he is an immortal monster who has killed more men than one can count.

Something has changed in him though. It's not that his edges have softened. Or that his power has diminished. If anything I think it's grown.

I think the difference in him has everything to do with James Hook.

"What is the 'usual stuff'?" he asks, and it takes me a minute to recall that we were talking about my nightmares.

I sigh. "Oh you know. Kidnappings. Prison. Hanging from a noose and the inevitable loneliness that comes when even Death forsakes you." I glance at him, hoping I've shocked him. But of course not. Can anything shock the Devourer of Men? He has heard and seen it all.

He gets up and crosses the room. He stops at the end of the bed and leans a shoulder against the far post, arms crossed over his chest. He's dressed himself, thank god. I don't think I could have a lucid conversation with him right now if he was shirtless, or worse, *naked*. "When did you first notice you couldn't be killed?"

I shrug. "It's not like one is faced with certain death on a regular basis."

"Speak for yourself," he says.

"Okay, well maybe *you* are. The first time I realized something was different about me was when I was sentenced to death and hung for treason. That was nearly a year after Pan left me here."

"And before then? Did you mysteriously avoid all illness? Did you heal quickly?"

I think over my childhood. "No, nothing like that. I nearly died from influenza when I was nine. I broke my wrist when I was twelve jumping over rocks in a nearby creek. My arm was in a cast for weeks and weeks."

"Did anything odd happen to you on Neverland? Or while in prison? Did anyone cut you? Did they give you a gift? Did you ever wake up having no recollection of how you got there?"

I frown at him. "No, why? What are you getting at?"

His gaze goes far away. "Well, I have a theory."

I sit up straighter. "About me?"

"Yes. And your abilities."

I wrap my arms around my knees. "What is it?"

He smiles at me, delighted to be asked, because there is nothing Roc loves more than unraveling secrets. "Well, I suspect that—"

The sound of clanging bells cuts him off, chiming through the castle and the surrounding grounds. A loud, discordant sound that sends a chill down my spine.

"Oh no." I climb up to my knees, then shimmy off the bed. "No. No. No."

Roc is at the window in an instant, yanking open the drapes. "No one is storming the castle. Which leaves—" He glances at me over his shoulder. I'm standing frozen in the center of the room. I've gone completely cold.

"The king is dead," I breathe out.

CHAPTER THIRTY

WENDY

I HURRY FROM ROC'S BEDROOM. THEY'LL BE LOOKING FOR ME now. They may already know I'm missing.

This isn't good.

It's very, very fucking bad.

"Wendy," Roc calls as he follows me out the door.

"Go find James and get out of this castle," I hiss at him over my shoulder. "It won't be safe here for you."

"And it is for you?" he counters.

I grumble to myself and turn the next corner and nearly run right into Asha and Theo.

To avoid crashing into them, I stumble back, but trip over my own feet and Roc has to catch me.

Theo's attention immediately goes to Roc's hands on my waist.

"There you are," Asha says.

"I know how this looks," I say. I don't want Theo turning on me now. Asha couldn't care less how I spend my nights, but Theo will.

"I was lost," Roc says. "I'm absolutely hopeless with directions."

Even though he's behind me, I can hear the self-depre-cating smile on his face.

Theo steps forward, putting his hand on my arm, steering me away from Roc. "Come, Your Majesty. We need to get you to a safe location."

"Of course. The king is..." I trail off, because I know how that sentence ends, but I want to hear it confirmed.

"Yes." Asha nods. "We should go."

Roc is suddenly in front of us. "I'm not leaving you now." Then he hastily adds, "Your Majesty."

"I'll be fine." Asha and Theo will have my back. "You have to go. You have to make sure James is okay."

He grumbles in frustration. He knows I'm right.

"Where will we find you?"

Asha and I share a glance. She was supposed to be working on an escape plan for me in the event of something disastrous. I would have to say the king dying is disastrous. Especially now with Roc and James here. Hally will be looking for any way to overthrow me, including murder.

"I'll send for you," Asha says. "When it's safe."

"Please," I tell Roc. "Go."

His jaw flexes and then he nods before turning in the opposite direction and disappearing around the next corner.

THEO AND ASHA GUIDE ME DOWN THE THIRD-FLOOR STAIRS AND then down a series of back hallways usually reserved for servants. I can immediately tell they're taking me to the unmarked, hidden exit on the west side of the castle. It'll be closest to the western supply gate. It's the easiest way out of the castle.

My heart thumps wildly the entire way there and I keep telling myself we'll make it, and Roc and James will make it, and everything will be okay.

But my stomach is churning and I think it's trying to tell me something.

Theo stops us at the end of one of those unused hallways and puts his finger to his lips.

The panic escalates.

"What is it?" Asha whispers. "I don't see—"

Theo pulls a thick, stubby baton from his belt and whacks Asha in the head.

I shout, then clamp my hand over my mouth.

Asha's eyes roll back and she crumples to her knees, blood flowing freely from a large split in her temple.

"Theo! Why did you do that?"

"She was working against you."

"What? Asha? No. That's not right."

Theo grabs my wrist and yanks me in the opposite direction.

I look back at Asha's unconscious body as Theo pulls me into the shadows.

Have I had it all wrong?

Every day I spent in this court, I questioned people's motives, whether or not they were using me, working against me, or worse, plotting against me. Never once did I question Asha.

Theo pulls me through a doorway that spills into a spiral stone staircase. Down, down we go.

"Where are we going?"

"You'll see," Theo tells me, his grip on me tightening. His pace is maddening and I'm barefoot and in my nightgown. I didn't dress for a clandestine escape.

The stairwell has no windows, only iron torches staked

into the stone, the flame flickering with every draft that steals in.

There is nothing in the stairwell to orient myself, and I realize too late that we aren't headed for an escape; we're below ground.

When the stairwell ends, it spills us into a narrow, low-ceiling tunnel. A tunnel that I know leads to the castle's dungeon.

The churning in my stomach magnifies until I fear I may vomit.

No.

There are three waiting guards at the end of the tunnel.

Theo yanks me forward, delivering me to them.

I bolt in the opposite direction, but Theo hooks me around the waist, lifting me off my feet. "No! I won't go. I won't go back!" I fight him with everything I have, but it's not enough. I was taken by surprise. Unprepared. Distracted. Naive.

Theo deposits me into the arms of the guards. It's three large, brawny men wearing leather uniforms that protect them from my flailing and clawing.

I'm screaming, feral. I can't breathe. I can't think. I just want to run. I want to run far and far and fast and far.

I won't go back.

I can't go back.

"Theo!" I shout. "Don't do this!"

"Apologies, Your Majesty," he says. "She paid me more than you ever could."

CHAPTER THIRTY-ONE

HOOK

WHAT AM I TO DO WITH THE CROCODILE'S CONFESSION?

What am I to make of myself now that I've had him, that he's shared his regrets?

He still took my hand and made a mockery of me all those years ago.

And I am still a disappointment to my father.

There was nothing the Commander held in higher regard than an upstanding man who did not cavort, who built a legacy with heirs to be proud of to continue on the illustrious Hook name.

I am none of those things. I am no upstanding man. I'm just a pirate with a legacy of a useless war against Peter Pan, and a family line that is now intertwined with him.

I keep giving in to my enemies. And I know what the Commander would think about it: *weak, you are weak and lacking fortitude.*

I stop in a rose garden planted in a half moon shape around a burbling fountain.

Hands on my hips, I look up at the stars.

I'm so bloody fucking confused.

All of my life, I have wanted to be what Commander William H. Hook wanted me to be. A good man. A father. A Hook with a legacy. But how can I build a legacy when I am chasing a married woman and an immortal beast who took my hand?

Shame churns in my gut.

As I stand there alone in the garden contemplating the wreckage of my life, bells toll through the castle.

It's such an odd sound in the dead of night that it raises the hair along my arms.

That surely cannot be good.

Shadows flit back and forth in front of the castle windows, the frenzy of the figures matching the loud clattering of the bells.

I hurry through the hedged path and return to the castle through a double door on the garden dining hall. There's no one here. Not that I'd expect it at this unholy hour. But I can hear footfalls and shouting coming from the grand foyer.

I make my way there and find the castle in chaos. Soldiers march through. Courtesans are in their robes, some of them crying. Servants are dashing up the stairs.

"What's happened?" I ask a woman shrouded in yards of red silk.

"A dreadful thing!" She clutches at my arm. "The king is dead!"

I follow another line of guards as they make their way up the grand staircase with the prince at the head.

"Bloody hell," I mutter.

The woman drops her mouth open, clearly offended at my language. Everland has become a kingdom of fucking prudes.

I need to get back to Wendy and Roc, but the main staircase is flooded with people. There's a back staircase—Roc and I were led up it after the prince invited us to stay, but I was exhausted and in shock. I can't remember how to reach it.

"Which way is the back staircase?" I ask the woman.

She frowns at me. "For illicit proceedings?"

"What? No. I...never mind." I'll find it myself.

I've been in enough grand houses to know that the back staircase is usually tucked in the back of the house near the kitchen. I turn into a dimly lit hallway that runs behind the grand staircase and run smack into a small, dark figure.

There is a bite across my arm, a sharp slicing motion.

"Oh gods!" a small voice says. "I'm so sorry."

When the woman comes into a circle of light cast from the wall sconce, I recognize her to be the prince's bride-to-be. She's clutching a bronze *sacrée*, the supposed weapon used to slaughter the *malum vermes* hundreds of years ago. It was crudely made, likely to look authentic to its medieval era. But that also means the end is sharp like a dagger.

And I think it's cut me.

"Many apologies, sir," she says again and grabs hold of my arm to inspect the damage. "My betrothed told me to escape to the safe room and this was the only weapon we had and—"

She's caught sight of the wound.

I know what she sees but I dare not look.

I am bleeding and I am bleeding black.

She gasps and staggers back two steps, then makes the mark of the X across her chest to ward off the dark spirits.

Meaning me.

"*Homme maléfique*," she hisses.

Evil man.

Fuck.

Of course I always knew this, didn't I? That I was made of dark things and darker urges. Especially true right now because I'm considering what it might take to kill her. Because now I've endangered Wendy. And Roc. With rumors already swirling in the castle about it being overrun by dark magic and dark witches, and with the prince already scheming against Wendy, his betrothed has been handed a golden arrow. I came here for Wendy and I am clearly cursed.

"There you are, Your Grace." A guard comes around the corner, spotting the bride-to-be. He senses the tension between us, sees the wide eyes of the girl and the way she's clutching the *sacrée* to her chest.

I shouldn't be here.

"Seize him!" she shouts.

I turn around and run.

CHAPTER THIRTY-TWO
ROC

I can't find the Captain anywhere.

Where the fuck did he run off to?

The panic is crowding in on me like an unwanted house guest.

I don't care if something happens to the Captain. So why the fuck does it feel like I do?

I pull out my pocket watch and check the time. The ticking of the secondhand is a comfort and a warning.

I am dangerously close to shifting.

I search the entire third floor of the castle, popping into rooms that are sometimes empty, sometimes not. Everyone is frustratingly unhelpful including the man that tried whacking me with an iron poker.

He howled like a cat when I drove it through his foot.

On the second floor, I check all of the sitting rooms, the ballrooms, other fucking rooms with no clear purpose other than to house more fucking chairs.

He is gone.

Did he leave me again?

I wander into a hallway off the main corridor and spot a

figure lying on the floor, blood pooled like a halo around a head of dark straight hair.

I think I know who it is, but I want to be sure it's not a trap.

I pause, listening for anyone nearby, but there is only the soft, steady thumps of a human heart.

I take another step.

That heartbeat sounds familiar.

When I reach the figure, I crouch down on a knee and examine her face.

This is the woman who Wendy walked away with. But she is also the woman who was eavesdropping on me in the kitchen—I recognize the pattern of her heart beat.

I'm impressed.

"Hey," I say and snap my fingers.

The girl lurches awake. In an impressive few seconds, she's behind me, one arm wrapped around my neck, the other locked over it.

"That won't work," I tell her, but my voice is stilted by the lack of air flow.

She says nothing, but I feel her unsteady balance, likely from a concussion.

"Why don't we talk like adults," I suggest.

She is still silent. I admire her tenacity.

I let the solid state of my body shift and my edges turn to wisps.

The girl gasps in surprise.

I take a fistful of her hair and vault her over my head. Her chokehold slips away and she thuds on her back on the floor, wheezing out air.

She rolls to all fours quickly, hacking, spitting.

"I did try to warn you," I tell her, rising to my feet. "What happened?"

"What?" She sucks in a deep breath.

"Who attacked you?"

She gets to her knees, sways, wipes at her mouth. Her gaze is distant but cutting.

"Why the fuck do you care?"

"Because last I saw you, you were with Wendy. Where is she now?"

The girl hurries to her feet. "Shit."

"Yes. What happened."

"He hit me. Theo."

"The guard?"

The girl nods.

"Where would he have taken her?"

"I honestly don't know. There are many options."

"Let's start with the most obvious."

She blinks several times like she's trying to think straight, then, "The dungeon."

I nod. "Show me."

CHAPTER THIRTY-THREE
WENDY

My vision blurs with the rising panic.

I don't want to go back.

I can't go back.

I fight and flail and thrash and scream.

But it's no use. There are three guards plus Theo. I'm no match for them. I will be thrown in the dungeon and I will rot there.

Tears spill over my eyes.

There is no one to save me.

The guards have me hooked between two of them, facing the way we came so that I'm being dragged backwards into the bowels of the castle. Theo trails behind us but he avoids looking directly at me.

We pass cell after cell. The air gets wetter, colder and I start to shiver.

I stop fighting and hang limp in their arms, sobbing, my bare feet bumping over the uneven rocky floor.

Maybe I was always destined to be forgotten in the dark. Maybe I was never meant to have any life at all. From the moment I was born, I knew I was cursed. I was always at the mercy of someone else.

I've very nearly given up, surrendering to my fate, when I hear the advice Asha once gave me burbling up from memory.

If you know how to properly knee a man in the balls, you will never be without a weapon.

I seize on that.

I have always admired Asha. For her strength, her intelligence, her bravery.

I have always wanted to be more like her.

You are not weak, she told me once when I complained about my ability to withstand court gossip. I know she meant that I was not mentally weak, but all this time she's been training me in the practice yard, she has given me another gift: confidence in my own strength.

I am not weak.

I will not be imprisoned.

I don't deserve it.

And more than that, I have fucking earned the right to *live*.

When the guards reach my assigned cell, the man at the front withdraws his ring of keys and opens the lock. The door creaks, the sound echoing through the tunnel.

Knowing I need a better position before they shove me into the cell, I go limp, dropping immediately to the floor. The uneven stone scrapes at my back, but I ignore the pain. Instead I use it as fuel.

"Christ," the man on my left says, grumbling to himself. "Leave her to me." He comes around, hooking his arms beneath mine, hoisting me up like a doll. "They say you're a witch but I think they got it wrong. Seems more like a petulant child to me."

The others laugh.

The man smells like ale and pickled cabbage. It makes my stomach roll.

With my feet beneath me and the man still in front of me, I brace myself to the stone, then put my hands on his shoulders the way Asha taught me.

Get a good foundation, she said. *Then control the body.*

Years and years and hours and hours of practice with Asha puts my body on autopilot.

I know what to do.

I send my knee flying upward. I hit the man square in the balls and he turns red on impact, all the air rushing out of him, spittle catching in his mustache. His eyes bulge as he shields himself from another attack, bending over like a wilting flower.

"Hey!" the other says.

"Grab her," the third says.

I yank the wilting man's dagger from his belt and spin around as the second guard charges toward me.

Always aim up, Asha said. *Most men will be taller than you. Vital organs will be higher. But watch for the ribs.*

The blade sinks easily into his flesh. Blood gushes down my arm.

I pull the blade out just as the third guard, the leader, grabs me by the shoulder and spins me around, his fist clenched, aimed for my face.

I duck. He punches air.

I sink the blade in his knee and his leg buckles. His howls bounce down the tunnel walls then come back.

Turn them into a pin cushion, Asha said once demonstrating on a stuffed potato sack. Boom. Boom. Boom.

Up. Aim.

I stab. Stab. Stab again.

The guard coughs up blood and crumples to the stone floor.

I heave a breath, adrenaline pumping through my veins as I stand in the middle of the carnage.

Then I turn around and face Theo.

His nostrils flare, eyes going big and round.

"You don't want to do this," he warns.

"Yes I very much do."

Blade still in hand, I charge him.

CHAPTER THIRTY-FOUR
HOOK

By some miracle, I make it out of the castle grounds unnoticed. The city inhabitants have clearly heard the bells and are now gathered at the main castle gate with candles and flowers, all while shouting and sobbing.

I fear for Everland's future, and for Wendy, but staying here will only endanger her more. I have to go. I have to go quickly.

All of the streets leading away from the castle are full of onlookers and mourners and I have to fight my way through.

I've just made it past a growing crowd when I hear crying. Not the soft sobbing of a mourner, but the frightened sniffles of a child.

I scan the surrounding intersection and spot a little boy huddled in a shop alcove, his coat torn, his face smudged with dirt and wet with tears.

There is no one else around.

I glance from the boy to the next street, the one that will take me directly to my ship.

"Bloody hell," I mutter and turn back for the shop alcove. "Are you lost?"

I don't know how old this boy is. Maybe four?

"Can you speak?" I try when he doesn't answer.

His eyes are red and watery, but the whimpers have ceased now that he's got sight of my hook.

Children hate the hook. I know it's frightening. And that's part of the reason I chose it. A pirate captain must be frightening if he means to get anywhere with his crew.

"It's all right," I tell him, putting the hook behind my back. "Are you looking for your mother?"

"Mommy," he says on a whimper, confirming my suspicions.

"All right. Up you go." Using my other arm, I scoop him up and set him on my hip. His tiny fingers curl into the lapel of my coat and he rests his head against my shoulder. "Which way is your mother?" I ask.

He points to the left. I have no time to waste so I hope he understands what I'm asking.

We go left. More people flow in from the city to the castle gates. I shield the little boy from their jostling and frenzy.

"Why do these people care so much if an old man dies?" I mutter and the little boy looks up at me with his big eyes and says nothing. "Pray to the gods you grow up with more sense."

"Henry!" a voice rings out over the crowd.

The little boy hiccups a breath.

"Is that your mother?" I ask him.

"Mommy," he whines.

"Henry!"

I follow the voice finding a woman in a threadbare

cloak, hands wringing in front of her as she searches the crowd.

"Henry!" she shouts when she spots the child on my hip. "Oh, my boy!"

The little boy starts sobbing harder and stretches out his arms for her. She takes him from me, wrapping him in a tight hug. Both of them cry together.

"Thank you," she says to me and squeezes my hand. "May the gods bless you. You are a good man. A good man who has done a good deed!"

"It's quite all right. No fuss necessary."

She yanks on a corded string tied around her neck, breaking it, and then hands it over to me. Dangling from the end is a pendant of a shining star. Most of the islands have some kind of religion. And most islands have some form of religion that considers the stars as gods.

"For you," the woman says, urging me to take it.

"I couldn't—"

She cuts me off, depositing the charm in my hand. "Yes. You must take it as a token of my thanks."

Then she tucks the boy beneath her chin and disappears around the next street corner.

I hold the necklace up to the light from a nearby lamppost. The charm spins back and forth, the star catching the golden light, then facing away again, to the dark.

You are a good man.

The words echo in my head.

A good man.

A good man.

Another crowd hurries past. I grab the nearest person and yank him to me. "Do you have a knife?"

"What?" He tries to shake me off but I'm determined now.

"A knife? Do you have one?"

His friends are pulling away from him. He looks from them to me and curses beneath his breath. "Here." He deposits a pocketknife in my hand. "It's cheap steel. Don't cut yourself with it." Then he's gone.

My stomach rolls.

I stuff the necklace in my pocket, then flick my wrist, and the blade pops open with a snap.

Am I really going to do this?

A good man who has done a good deed.

Roc challenged my belief about my blood. I have to know if he's right.

I put the sharp edge of the blade against the underside of my arm, just below the leather strap that keeps my hook attached to my arm.

"Here goes," I whisper, feeling like I might already vomit.

With a short, sharp pull, the blade cuts through my flesh. My vision tunnels, my head swaying. But I manage to stay conscious and look down at the blood welling in the cut.

It's black.

There is no difference whether I do a good deed or a vile one.

My father tricked me.

"Bloody hell," I say through gritted teeth and change direction.

Roc was right.

CHAPTER THIRTY-FIVE
HOOK

Making my way back to the castle takes twice as much effort as escaping it. But I still manage because when I'm determined to do something, I fucking do it.

I don't care if Wendy is still technically married to a dead king. If she wants to leave this place, I will take her wherever she wants to go. She deserves to finally have a life of her own choosing. Roc can come too if he'd like. If he behaves himself.

I'm so overwhelmed by the realization that my blood doesn't automatically mean I am bad, that I nearly run into the prince's bride-to-be *again*.

But something has changed.

She's smiling at me.

"You came back," she says, hands folded in front of her.

The timid, slightly scandalized girl of before is gone, replaced with something knowing and more menacing.

From the moment I first met her, I thought she was familiar, but I couldn't place her.

But as I stare at her and really take in the tiny, sharp

nose, the hollow cheeks, the wide set eyes and wavy brown hair, it comes to me.

She was different back then.

Her hair had been longer and braided into two braids. Her dark eyes had been lined in dark kohl. She was not adorned in royal jewels, but instead wore thick braided rope around her neck with shells woven in.

The truth of the matter hits me so squarely that it makes my head spin.

"You're the witch in the woods," I say. "The one my father took me to see."

Her smile widens and as she does, her chin turns down, her eyes narrowing.

"How...why..."

"Why am I here?" she says for me. "*How* am I here?" she adds. "Would you like the whole story? Or just the important bits?"

I clench my jaw. "The whole story."

"Very well. Follow me." She turns down the main corridor on the first floor.

I glance over my shoulder. The castle has quieted since I left it earlier, but there is still shouting in the recess. The sun is beginning to rise and light flares through the high windows of the mezzanine.

Do I dare go with her?

It occurs to me that this woman may be a parasite infiltrating Wendy's court. There were whispers of magic and witches. I know Wendy is mortal. So it stands to reason the rumors are actually about *this* woman.

But she's also connected to my past and to who I thought I was.

Perhaps it's no coincidence that she's here now, our paths crossing just when I've started to question everything my father made me believe about myself using her as part of the scheme.

I decide to follow her.

emerald green and the drapes are toile green to match. She pours herself a drink and offers me one. To be cautious, I watch her sip from hers before taking a swig of mine.

It's a sweet wine, reminiscent of fairy wine, but with far too much tartness. It overwhelms the burn of the alcohol.

"I am originally from Lostland," she tells me. "The home of the Myth Makers."

One of the Isles' secret societies, the ones always working behind the scenes for power and prestige and wealth.

"I did a bad thing once." She brings her arm across her middle, the glass still held in hand. "The Myth Makers are controlled by a council of seven. They are known as the Myths and at one point, I was to be inducted as one. But the oldest Myth thought I was too, *well*, feral, and he bypassed me for his nephew. So I killed him. The nephew, not the Myth. That didn't go over well." She laughs to herself and begins to pace the room.

I'm not sure what to do with myself. I'm still shocked she's here. I'm still shocked she somehow managed to make herself the prince's betrothed and then hid in plain sight looking the part of a demure bride-to-be.

But why? Why is she here and what does that have to do with me?

"I was banished from Lostland and the Seven Isles," she goes on. "I was thrown into the mortal realm and not only was I banished, but I was blocked from finding my way back to the Isles. No matter how hard I looked, no matter what magic I did, I couldn't go back."

She makes her way around a green settee with an ornate gilded frame. "I established myself as a mystic in your realm, but every day my magic waned. Disconnected from the Isles, it was like my magic was blocked too. I became desperate to try anything. The mortal realm is starving for magic, but you can find the right people if you know where to look.

"I visited a fortune teller and asked for her guidance, and she told me the way back was by the hook."

She paces to the window and sips from her wine. "I was confused at first. What does that even mean? Months I researched and analyzed and fretted over it. Until a man darkened my door asking me to teach his misbehaving son a lesson. The man's name was William H. Hook."

I suspected this was where her story would lead but still hearing my father's name spoken after all this time, by someone other than me, pulls up all of my repressed memories of him.

I hated the man and loved him equally. I worked hard for his respect. I worked harder to meet his standards. But it was never enough. And I think deep down I knew that whatever his standards were, they were impossible to reach because they were always moving, always changing.

The witch goes on. "It was a coin toss as to whether William or James—" she tilts her glass toward me "—were the subject of the fortune teller's prediction, so I took a gamble and chose you. Your father wanted me to fix you, but I just needed a map. So using what little power I had left, I gave you a part of myself, the most important part: my magic."

I instinctively glance down at the cut on my arm, now crusted over black.

"You set sail one day and you never returned," she says. "Because of course you quite literally stumbled into the Seven Isles when I had been searching for my way through for decades. But once you were there, all I had to do was track my magic and follow you." She spreads out her arms. "Voila. I am home. But what I didn't account for is that you would impregnate a Darling and that the Darling baby would give its mother power too."

My mouth drops open.

That explains Wendy's ability to heal. And it begs the question: was the power continually passed down through the familial line? Does Winnie Darling have some power inherited from the Myth Makers?

I take another sip from the wine to settle my nerves. This is so much to take in. "Now you are here," I say to the witch. "What do you want of Everland?"

She smiles. "The Myth I told you about? The one who banished me? He's dead now. A new Myth reigns and plans are in motion. I am just a cog in the scheme."

"Bloody hell."

"Oh yes, Captain Hook," she says and tips her glass to me. "It will be bloody indeed."

I have to find Roc and tell him what I've learned. I have to save Wendy before the Myth Makers turn this entire court into a battlefield.

I set my glass on one of the tables and make my way for the door. But turning abruptly makes the room spin. At first I think it may be lack of sleep or perhaps hunger. But standing still doesn't help it abate.

The witch's footsteps come closer. I stumble forward, crash into the table. The glass wobbles, then spills over and as the liquid drips to the floor, I notice it's speckled with something green.

My knees give out and I crash to the floor.

"Sorry, Captain Hook." The witch crouches beside me. "I would like my magic back now if I'm to help the Myth Makers take over all seven of the isles."

CHAPTER THIRTY-SIX

WENDY

I'M LOSING THIS FIGHT.

Theo knows me better than the other guards. He's countering every one of my moves and when his fist catches me across the jaw, blood fills my mouth, stars blinking in my eyes. The force of the blow spins me around and I stumble to the stone on my knees.

Get up! I scream at my aching, exhausted body. *Get up!*

"Wendy. Wendy. Wendy." Theo clucks his tongue as he ambles over. "I had really hoped you'd make this easier on yourself."

"Who paid you, Theo?" I scramble to my feet. "Don't you know you can't trust any of them?"

He smiles. Watery blood is coating his teeth. "Maybe you can't trust the witch, but she's already given me twice what you have in gold. Did you really expect me to believe you when you said you'd marry me once the old man died? It was easy to say yes to the witch when she propositioned me."

"What witch? What are you talking about?"

"Mareth," he finally says. "Mareth is the witch."

Hally's betrothed? That doesn't seem right. She's so quiet. So timid.

But of course now that I think of it, isn't that the perfect way to hide in plain sight?

God I've been so oblivious. Too focused on my own misery to notice there was someone scheming right in front of my face.

"What does Mareth want?" I ask as Theo circles me in the tunnel. "What does she stand to gain?"

"Power," Theo admits and then he lunges for me.

He gets his hand around my throat and drives me back against the wall. When I hit the stone, the force of the blow knocks the wind out of me and pain lances through my ribs.

I choke on the need for oxygen.

Theo wrenches the dagger from my grip and then turns it on me.

Still gasping for air, I block his advance, crossing my forearm in front of his.

But I'm not strong enough to fight him hand to hand for long.

The sharp end of the dagger gets closer and closer to my chest.

Theo grits his teeth, pushes forward.

If he strikes, he'll pierce through my heart and I'll be dead. I don't exactly know what I'm fighting for anymore, but I know I don't want to die.

There's only one option.

I have to control the outcome.

I drop my stance, sinking down the stonewall while at the same time letting up on the block against Theo.

Withdrawing my opposition takes him by surprise and the dagger plows forward, hitting me in the shoulder instead of the heart.

He growls in frustration, but the sound is distant, like I'm underwater.

The pain is nearly insurmountable.

It blows through my shoulder, down my neck, vibrating down my spine.

My mouth forms a cry but no sound comes out. The pain has stolen all the air from my lungs.

It's only seconds later, when a breath manages to trickle in, that a wailing screech makes it past my lips.

"Shut the fuck up," Theo says and winds back his hand to slap me.

"I wouldn't do that if I were you."

Theo comes to a sudden halt.

Roc emerges from the shadow in the tunnel's natural curve. Behind him is Asha, blood crusted on her forehead.

Theo smirks but anyone with two eyes could see the fear etched around his mouth.

"She attacked me," Theo says. "She's gone absolutely crazy."

"You know," Roc says as he comes forward with slow, lazy steps, "I made myself a promise when you barged into our room at the inn, when you hit my Captain."

"Oh yeah?" Theo takes a step back as if the way to keep himself safe is to keep a distance between himself and Roc.

"I promised myself that at the first opportunity, I'd fucking kill you."

Theo laughs. "I was just doing my job."

"Sure. Sure." Roc takes a few more steps. Flame from the torches embedded in the wall skim him in flickering light. "Then, after you arrested us and dragged us in front of the queen, you hit me with your baton. Do you remember?"

Theo runs his tongue along his teeth. "Not particularly."

"I made myself a second promise. That you were double dead."

"What the—"

Roc reaches back, steals Asha's dagger from her hip and sends it sailing through the air. The blade hits Theo in the throat and blood geysers from the wound.

Theo blinks wide-eyed and pale.

Then Roc darts forward, almost a blur, and takes Theo's head between his two hands and twists.

CRACK.

Theo's face is turned away from his body at an unnatural angle.

He drops to the floor like a sack of sticks.

"There," Roc says and dusts off his hands. "Double dead."

Asha comes over to me. "Are you okay?"

I hold my injured arm close to my side. "I think so."

Roc asks, "Can you walk?"

"Yes."

"Then we should go."

"What about James?"

Asha and Roc share a look. "We haven't found him yet," Roc admits. "I was looking for him when I found your friend."

My heart sinks. I push away from the wall and grimace as pain burns through my shoulder.

"Don't take it out," Roc warns.

"Here." Asha comes forward and rips a length of fabric from the bottom of my nightgown leaving it tattered and hitting just above my knees. She takes the strip and winds it around the dagger and my shoulder stabilizing the weapon.

I squeeze my eyes shut the entire time, worried that if I don't, I might pass out.

"Better?" Asha asks.

I give her a grim nod. It's as good as it's going to get for now.

Roc comes over and hooks his arm around my waist, pulling me into him. He drapes my arm over his shoulders, holding on to my hand to keep me anchored. "If you need me to carry you, tell me."

"I'll be fine. Really."

"No," he says and looks down at me. "You'll tell me." It's not hard to know when Roc is giving a command and not a suggestion. His default state is all charm. Anything other than that is not to be ignored.

"Fine. I'll tell you."

"Good. Now let's move."

CHAPTER THIRTY-SEVEN
WENDY

When we make it above ground, I breathe a little easier and the pain in my shoulder subsides. But every step saps more and more energy from my body and by the time we're passing the kitchen, I'm leaning heavily on Roc.

"Where was James going when he left your room?" I ask Roc.

"He didn't say."

"We're never going to find him."

"Yes we will."

He sounds so sure.

Roc stops in the center of the foyer, his eyes going unfocused.

"What is it?"

"Sounds," he mutters, narrowing his eyes to concentrate. "There are guards coming in a side entrance. Somewhere behind us."

"I'm on it," Asha says.

"Wait! Alone?"

She jogs backwards as she says, "They don't call me Bonescar for nothing."

"She's incredibly loyal to you," Roc observes as he guides us forward again.

"We're loyal to one another."

"I'm glad you have her."

"Me too."

We make it down the east corridor before Roc stops us again.

I groan from a slice of pain.

"Shhh," he orders.

I scowl up at him, but do as he says, damn near holding my breath.

"I can hear him," Roc finally says and then he's racing forward, towing me beside him.

We spill into the grand foyer.

Hally is there along with Merath and several of the guard.

We're not quiet, by any means, and our shuffling over the marble floor pulls Hally's attention. He immediately looks surprised to see me.

So it is true. Theo wasn't lying about Mareth paying him to imprison me, and maybe she even did it at the prince's behest. Mareth and her powers must be how Hally stopped aging. And if I had to guess, it probably had something to do with the king suddenly becoming ill, and my not being able to save him. They were working against me the entire time and I had no idea.

In the center of the foyer, swaying on his knees, eyes heavy, is James.

"What did you do to him?" Roc asks.

"He has something that belongs to me," Mareth answers.

It's almost startling, her transformation from meek, quiet bride-to-be, to clearly the one in charge.

"If it's something he can give, he'll give it," Roc says.

"I can't," Hook mumbles.

"What is it?" I ask.

"It doesn't belong to him," Mareth goes on. "So he has no right to keep it."

"What is *it*?" I ask again.

Mareth turns to face me, hands clasped in front of her. "Part of my power."

"Myth Maker power," Roc adds.

Mareth's gaze cuts to Roc. She says nothing, which I think is all the confirmation I need.

I only vaguely remember reading about the secret societies in the library one night while Asha worked on a translation. According to the book, there are many societies in the Isles, but The Myth Makers are one of the most powerful and mysterious. It doesn't help that they're based in Lostland, the only island no one can point to on a map.

"How long has he had this power?" I ask still hanging from Roc's side.

"Longer than he's known you."

It's not hard to connect the dots. There's an entire section in the castle library on the transference of power through bindings, pregnancies, plagues, and blood oaths.

Which means James had part of this power when I got pregnant.

Which means...

"What does this power do?" I slip out of Roc's grasp and I hear him grumble as I do. "Would it make someone invincible? Would it give them the ability to heal?"

Mareth smiles at me. "It could, yes."

I should feel relief that the mystery of my own power has been solved. But it just makes my stomach churn with anxiety.

The consequences of having Myth Maker power must be numerous. And furthermore, if the baby had power, then the entire Darling line starting with me is part of the Myth Makers.

I can't even wrap my head around that right now. Not while there's a knife stuck in my shoulder and James is on his knees in front of the witch that began this entire thing.

"Whatever the power," Roc says coming up behind me. "Can it be removed without hurting the Captain?"

Mareth frowns, but there is nothing in her demeanor that says she's sympathetic. "I'm afraid not."

"Then you're not getting it back." Roc pushes forward, but several guards step in front of him, swords and armor clattering as they draw their weapons.

Roc smiles at them, running his tongue over his sharp incisors.

"I'm sorry, Crocodile. You'll have to find some other pirate to warm your bed." Mareth pulls a *sacrée* from a sheath strapped at her hip.

"No!" I shout.

James sways when he sees the weapon as if his mind is trying to tell his body to move, but it won't follow through.

I turn to Roc to beg him to do something, but he's already a blur racing across the foyer.

CHAPTER THIRTY-EIGHT
ROC

Tick-tock.

Tick-tock.

I don't have to think about what I'm about to do. Whatever the consequences, they'll be worth it.

The line of guards between me and the Captain is twenty-wide, but that's at least fifty fewer than they'd need to stop me.

I target the guy in the middle, the one with the trembling grip and sweaty brow.

I hit him with my shoulder. He flies back easily and slams to the floor with an umph. I wrench the sword from his grip and close the rest of the distance between me and the witch in the span of a breath.

Her crude blade hits my stolen sword with a clang.

Her nostrils flare, her gaze meeting mine in surprise.

"*Mine*," I tell her.

The ticking gets louder in my head.

Tick-tock.

Tick-tock.

It's time the Crocodile came out to play.

CHAPTER THIRTY-NINE
HOOK

I'M NOT SURE IF I'LL EVER GET USED TO WATCHING THE Crocodile transform.

One minute he is man, the next his edges are made of darkness and mist.

He devours the witch whole.

The prince is rendered stupid, watching it happen, then he's sputtering orders and the guards make a valiant effort defending the castle against the Devourer of Men.

It doesn't take Roc long to make his way through the line.

Their screams echo through the foyer and up around the mezzanine filling the castle with terror and carnage.

Bone by bone, Roc devourers them all and everyone in the foyer is powerless to stop him.

When it's over, his formless silhouette is before me, two glowing yellow eyes in bottomless darkness.

"Captain," he says in a voice that is ancient and chilling, and then he's man again, collapsing into my arms.

We go down together. He's dead weight, somehow

heavier than he's ever been even though his size hasn't changed.

"Monster," the prince starts, then his voice gains volume. "Monster!" He charges at Roc, blade drawn.

I squirm under Roc's weight, trying to get my feet out.

I don't know if he can withstand a knife wound. I don't know the rules of a beast but I don't want to find out.

I manage to get out from beneath him and instinctively reach for my pistols before remembering I don't have them and haven't since they arrested us.

I scan the surroundings, spotting the witch's abandoned *sacrée.*

I scramble for it as the prince charges.

Wendy rushes forward and careens with the prince. They clatter to the floor. The prince loses his blade. He gets up on all fours and slips over the bloody marble to retrieve it.

With the *sacrée* in a firm grip, I stalk over to the prince. I don't really know anything about him other than he wants to kill Roc. That's all I need to know.

The prince gets the blade and messily climbs to his feet, his balance unsteady on the wet floor.

When he turns around, he slips in the blood again and I take the opportunity to introduce him to the crude point of the *sacrée.*

He spills forward, stumbling into me, his blood splashing down my front.

I shake him off and he falls over, eyes watery with unshed tears as the life drains out of him.

THE FIRST RAYS OF SUNLIGHT FLARE IN THROUGH THE WINDOWS.

I look over at Wendy clutching at her shoulder where a blade is sticking out of her.

Beyond the castle, shouting of the townspeople has reached a crescendo.

"We need to get Roc to my ship," I tell her and she nods.

I grab Roc beneath the arms and Wendy tries to grab his feet, but her left arm, the one with the blade protruding from her shoulder, is pretty much useless.

Wendy drops him and grits her teeth against a wave of pain.

"It's okay," I tell her. "I can drag him." Except whatever drug the witch gave me is still making its way through my system. Every time I look directly at Wendy, I see her in double.

"We don't have time for that." Wendy curses beneath her breath and sucks back tears. "Maybe we—"

A girl jogs into the foyer. She's covered in blood, as if she fought her way through a slaughterhouse.

"Asha!" Wendy calls. "Thank god."

The girl comes over and surveys the situation.

"I can't lift him," Wendy explains.

"What's wrong with him?"

"He does this," I tell the girl. "He'll be out for a few days. We have to get him to my ship."

The girl, Asha, nods. "I can help you if you have room for one more on that ship."

Wendy and I share a look. Does she trust this girl? The expression on her face leads me to believe she'd beg for the girl's company whether she helped or not.

"Of course," I tell her. "You help us get him to safety, I'll take you wherever you want to go."

I carry Roc beneath the arms while Asha takes his legs, leading the way out. She guides us through the castle to an unloading dock where an empty hand cart is letting off steam in the early morning sun.

"Was this always your plan for me?" Wendy asks Asha. "Stuffing me in a handcart?"

"It's as good as any other escape."

"Not as dignified," Wendy mutters and Asha laughs.

We deposit Roc inside. I don't think he'd have the same opinion as Wendy about being carted off like a sack of potatoes. He'd probably love it. He'd only love it more if it was a royal litter.

At Asha's suggestion, we've put on cloaks belonging to delivery boys while hiding Roc beneath a pile of hay.

No one stops us on the way out and when the castle is far behind us, and we pause to catch our breath, I turn to the women. "What will come of the court now?"

Asha bites off a piece of dried meat and then hands the rest to Wendy. "Eat," she orders and Wendy takes the snack eagerly.

"To be perfectly fair," Asha says, "the Everland court has been in need of a reset for a very long time."

Wendy rips off a strip of the dried meat with her teeth. "She's right. I helped Hald hold onto power much longer than he should have. There were rumblings. It's going to be messy before it gets better. I don't know who will fill the void left by the Grimmaldi family and I don't really care."

More bells chime through the city.

"I have my suspicions," Asha says and nods at a creaking wooden sign across the street.

I realize we've come up on The Tipping Well.

"The fae?" I guess.

"They've secretly been buying up property here for

years. You can see their fingerprints all over the city records if you look deep enough."

Perhaps the city could use that same calming energy I experienced in the tavern.

Good leadership can make all the difference. The question is, will the fae want peace or power?

WHEN WE FINALLY MAKE IT BACK TO MY SHIP, MY SISTER, CHERRY is there waiting for us on the deck.

"I was almost going to come looking for you," she says.

"Cherry?" Wendy shouts.

"Wendy Darling?!"

The two women collide in a hug. Wendy lets out a groan of pain before Cherry steps back realizing she's injured.

Asha and I struggle getting Roc up the plank on the handcart, but together we finally get him over the edge and onto the deck.

"I didn't know you were here!" Wendy says to my sister.

"Jas made me stay on the ship." Cherry cuts me an annoyed look. "I've about run out of wine, Jas."

"Apologies, Cherry. It isn't like we were fighting for our lives or anything." I remove the hay from the cart exposing Roc.

Though he's been rendered unconscious, he is no less monstrous.

But he's my monster now.

With Asha's help, we get him into my bedroom as my men ready the ship. I'm exhausted but I want to get as far away from here as possible. When my new quartermaster asks where to set sail to, I tell him, "Anywhere but Neverland." The next closest islands are Pleasureland and Dark-land and either will do as far as I'm concerned.

When the anchor is pulled and we set sail, I finally relax, pulling a chair up beside my bed. One of my men brings me roasted meat and a bottle of rum and a sweet smelling cigar.

I take a bit of the meal but the food sits like a weight in my stomach. I drown it out with rum.

Wendy comes in sometime later freshly dressed and her wound tended to.

"How is he?" she asks and gingerly sits down on the end of the bed.

Outside, the waves lap softly against the hull. It's a glorious day for a voyage. I wish I could properly enjoy it, but I don't think I'll feel settled until Roc wakes up.

"He hasn't stirred," I tell her. "Vane said they're usually out for several days. We're to mix blood and water and pour it down his throat."

"Vane." Wendy laughs to herself. "I'd completely forgotten about him. How is that asshole?"

"He tried to kill Cherry."

"He what?"

"She put the other Darling in a compromising position and—"

Wendy's eyebrows lift. "The other Darling?"

I meet her eyes. There's so much she doesn't know, so much she has to catch up on. "It's a long story. Perhaps for another time."

She sighs and rubs at her eyes. There are dark rings beneath, and her skin is paler than normal from blood loss.

"Why don't you get some rest?" I tell her.

She blinks and nods to herself. "Maybe I will." She gets up from the bed.

"No," I tell her, cutting her off. "Here. I'm not letting you out of my sight." I glance at Roc. "Neither of you."

Wendy gives me a weak smile. "You were always the best of us, James."

"I'm just a pirate who—"

She comes over and swallows my objection with a kiss. Warmth spreads through my chest.

"You are not just a pirate," she says. "You are one of the most caring men I've ever met."

For the first time in my life, I believe it to be true.

The ship follows the swell of a wave and Wendy jostles in my arms. She laughs. I hoist her up and pat her on the ass. "Off to bed with you."

I guide her into the bed beside Roc where she curls into his side. I pull the blanket up for her, tucking her in.

And before long, she's sleeping too.

WENDY AND ROC SLEEP SOUNDLY, BOTH OF THEM UNMOVING FOR hours and hours.

I doze in my chair at the bedside as night descends on the ocean. The sway of the ship on the waves is a comfort I didn't realize I needed.

For one blinding moment, I am happy and content.

EPILOGUE
HOOK

I LURCH AWAKE SURROUNDED BY DARKNESS.

I stumble to one of the oil lamps and light it with a match. A flickering gold light fills my quarters.

I grab a nearby glass of unfinished rum and sling it back, then turn to the bed to check on Wendy and Roc.

Except there is only one figure curled in the sheets.

Where is Roc? How long has it been? He shouldn't be awake yet.

Beyond my quarters, there is a crash, then a thud.

I hurry down the hall. The ship heaves over a wave and I bang against the wall.

Another crash.

When I emerge in the dining room, I find Roc hunched over a table and on the floor is one of my men—or rather, *half of one.*

"What the bloody hell is going on?"

The ship rolls again. I widen my stance, bracing myself. Several dishes fall from the table, shattering on the floor.

Roc rights himself. His eyes are glowing yellow.

"What are you doing?" I yell at him.

"Captain."

"You can't go around eating my men!"

"Captain," he says again.

"What?!"

He flashes to his beastly form, then back to his solid form.

I surge forward once the ship rights itself, but when I grab Roc by the arm, he disintegrates in my grip like he's nothing but ocean mist.

"Something is wrong," he rasps and then shifts again.

The ship crests a wave and Roc stumbles toward me, but he goes right *through* me like a ghost.

I turn around just in time to see him re-solidify and crash into a table. When I come up on him, he's blurred again, but there is a face swirling in his mist.

The Myth Maker witch.

Christ.

"What's happening?" I ask again.

He clutches at my jacket, his yellow eyes wide.

There is terror in his gaze.

"What do I do?" I ask him, desperate for something, desperate to save him.

I can feel him shaking as if he can't quite hold himself together.

"I need Vane. I need my brother. Take me—" He sucks in a breath. "Take me back to Neverland."

I hope you enjoyed reading Devourer of Men! Writing Roc and Hook was an absolute joy, and as always, writing women like Wendy and Asha is not only a joy but a pleasure.

There's still more to come for these characters. And we may just see a few familiar characters pop back up in book 2.

If you'd like to stay up-to-date, I highly recommend subscribing to my newsletter or joining Patreon (there is a free option on Patreon!):

To sign-up for my newsletter, scan the QR code below:

Or join Patreon here:
https://www.patreon.com/nikkistcrowe

ALSO BY NIKKI ST. CROWE

DEVOURER

Devourer of Men

VICIOUS LOST BOYS

The Never King

The Dark One

Their Vicious Darling

The Fae Princes

WRATH & RAIN TRILOGY

Ruthless Demon King

Sinful Demon King

Vengeful Demon King

Wrath & Reign Omnibus

HOUSE ROMAN

A Dark Vampire Curse

MIDNIGHT HARBOR

Hot Vampire Next Door (ongoing Vella serial)

Hot Vampire Next Door: Season One (ebook)

Hot Vampire Next Door: Season Two (ebook)

Hot Vampire Next Door: Season Three (ebook)

Ink & Feathers

ABOUT THE AUTHOR

NIKKI ST. CROWE has been writing for as long as she can remember. Her first book, written in the 4th grade, was about a magical mansion full of treasure. While she still loves writing about magic, she's ditched the treasure for something better: villains, monsters, and anti-heroes, and the women who make them wild.

These days, when Nikki isn't writing or daydreaming about villains, she can either be found on the beach or at home with her husband and daughter.

NEWSLETTER SIGN-UP
www.subscribepage.com/nikkistcrowe

FOLLOW NIKKI ON INSTAGRAM
www.instagram.com/nikkistcrowe

JOIN NIKKI'S FACEBOOK GROUP
www.facebook.com/groups/nikkistcrowesnest

VISIT NIKKI ON THE WEB AT:
www.nikkistcrowe.com

facebook.com/authornikkistcrowe

instagram.com/nikkistcrowe

tiktok.com/@nikkistcrowe

amazon.com/author/nikkistcrowe

bookbub.com/profile/nikki-st-crowe

Made in the USA
Las Vegas, NV
05 November 2024

11199605R00142